*H*ey, Officer Winter," Zach piped up. "I was wondering if I could ask you something."

"Sure, Zach. Ask away." Lee Winter had beautiful hands for a man. Cassie could see them next to her when she looked down at her lunch tray and enjoyed the long, slender fingers and the sprinkle of brown-gold hair there. No rings or jewelry to distract her, except for a plain watch in a brushed silver finish.

"It's my mom's birthday next week and me an' Sarah want to get her something really cool. If we paid, would you take her out to dinner?"

Cassie's surprise was so great that her carefully balanced forkful of salad slid into her lap. It was a moment before she could say anything. When she did, the words were clipped and precise. "Zachary Jonathan Neel, you are grounded. For life."

Palisades.
Pure Romance.

FICTION THAT FEATURES CREDIBLE CHARACTERS AND
ENTERTAINING PLOT LINES, WHILE CONTINUING TO UPHOLD
STRONG CHRISTIAN VALUES. FROM HIGH ADVENTURE
TO TENDER STORIES OF THE HEART, EACH PALISADES
ROMANCE IS AN UNDILUTED STORY OF LOVE,
FROM BEGINNING TO END!

A PALISADES CONTEMPORARY
ROMANCE

Surrender

Lynn Bulock

PALISADES

SURRENDER
published by Palisades
a division of Multnomah Publishers, Inc.

© 1997 by Lynn Bulock
Published in association with the literary agency of Writer's House, Inc.
21 W. 26th Street, New York, NY 10010.

International Standard Book Number: 0-57673-104-9

Cover illustration by Glenn Harrington
Cover designed by Brenda McGee

Printed in the United States of America

For information:
MULTNOMAH PUBLISHERS, INC.
POST OFFICE BOX 1720
SISTERS, OREGON 97759

97 98 99 00 01 02 03 04 — 10 9 8 7 6 5 4 3 2 1

To Joe, always

*And to the wonderful "ladies of the loop," past and present,
especially Annie J, for the encouragement, and Kasey, who
urged me to write when I just wanted to sit and eat worms.*

*Be kind and compassionate to one another, forgiving each other,
just as in Christ God forgave you.*

EPHESIANS 4:32, NIV

Prologue

"It's a lie. It's got to be a lie," Cassie Neel murmured to herself, sitting cross-legged in the middle of her living-room floor. Tears streamed down her face, and she wondered if any part of her seven-year marriage had ever been based on the truth. The last year or two hadn't been, that was for sure. Not judging by Brad's letter in her hand.

As a college professor he didn't travel much, except to a conference once in a while. If he'd seemed more nervous or distant than usual packing for this one, it wasn't apparent to her. Cassie racked her brain, thinking of some sign, some warning that would have clued her in to the bombshell he dropped in the letter he left.

If it had been there, she'd missed it in running after a preschooler and a toddler. Of course, she reflected, as she wiped tears from her face, that was part of the problem according to Brad. That she was always busy with Sarah and Zach. That she'd become a boring, frumpy housewife and mother instead of the interesting woman he married.

She looked down at the wrinkled paper. It wasn't even handwritten. Instead, the paper bore the marks of being torn out of Brad's printer in his office at the college. Trust him to protect himself from delivering such news himself.

> *Dear Cassie,*
> *By the time you read this, I will be gone. I won't be coming back Sunday night as planned. In fact, I won't be coming back at all. Since the rumors will eventually reach you anyway, I might as well tell you why: I've met someone new.*
> *Our marriage has become increasingly stultifying. I can't imagine spending the rest of my life in such a dead relationship, not when I have the choice of being with someone vibrant and alive. A choice I had no trouble making.*
> *My attorney will contact you soon about settlement details.*
> *Bradley*

Stultifying? Vibrant? she murmured to herself. They sounded like words out of one of his lectures, Cassie thought, as she crumbled the paper into a ball. Then she covered her face with her hands and wept.

When the doorbell rang, Cassie didn't move. Even when it rang again, it took a few minutes to rise off the carpet and walk slowly to the front door. She opened the door and moved back with surprise.

What was a policeman doing on her front porch? And when had it started raining?

"Mrs. Neel?" the young man asked.

"Yes?" Cassie opened the door wider, staring at the young officer. He wore rain gear, but it wasn't protecting him much from the elements. Rain streamed down from his billed hat and came off his poncho in sheets.

"I'm Officer Lee Winter. Missouri Highway Patrol. May I come in?"

Cassie shook her head, trying to clear it enough to think what she should do. "Of course. I don't know what I was thinking."

The officer stepped in on the hall rug. His blue eyes were clouded. "I'm sorry about making all this mess."

"You can't help it," Cassie assured him.

He looked around, those eyes still filled with a pain that seemed far deeper than was necessary for messing up her rug. "Is there someone here with you?"

Cassie felt a chill of fear. What had she done, letting a total stranger into her house like this, even if he was a police officer? "N-not really," she stammered. "Just the children. And they're asleep."

"Mrs. Neel, I don't know how to start this. It's the first time I've had to do this," the officer said. He swallowed hard, then went on. "Your husband Bradley has been in a traffic accident on the highway, heading toward Columbia. There was a truck that lost control of its brakes. He…I'm sorry." He halted, looking at Cassie while her foggy brain fought to understand what he was saying.

"Bradley? In an accident? Is he in the hospital?" Cassie's mind reeled. What an evil joke that would be, if all Brad's plans to leave her had to be put on hold while he recovered from injuries in an accident.

"No, he isn't. He's…he didn't make it," the officer said. "He died immediately." Then he paused, his expression kind. "Is there someone you can call, someone to come over and be with you right now?"

"No," Cassie said, looking down at the spreading puddle in the hall under the police officer's wet black shoes. "Not locally, anyway." She shuddered as she shook her head. "There's no one."

The officer seemed reluctant to leave, but once he was sure Cassie understood everything he was telling her, he did, finally,

13

after promising that someone from the department would call Brad's mother. Cassie wouldn't have to be the one to break such horrible news to the older woman.

Then he was gone, leaving behind only that puddle. She stared at it for an hour after he left, trying to find the energy to get a towel and mop it up before she had to start making phone calls.

In the morning she tried to explain things to the children. Of course they didn't understand. At twenty-four months, Zachary's favorite word had become "Daddy." And at five years old, the only death Sarah had ever faced was that of her goldfish. This was too much for them to comprehend. When Cassie left them with the next-door neighbor so that she could go to the bank for the documents she needed, they were playing with blocks, blissfully unaware.

When she got to the bank, Cassie told herself that things could only get better. Or at least easier. Surely all the horrible, mindless details she'd face in the next few days would keep her from thinking about what was happening. It was stifling in the little room where she took the safe-deposit box. She hadn't been here for years, since she and Brad rented the box together and put in a few things. She knew that Brad visited it regularly. What would she find? The question made her feel tense and dizzy. It was almost as if she watched as a detached spectator as her hand reached out and opened the lid. Her hands shook as she lifted it and started riffling through all the documents.

The box was filled with papers. There was Bradley's life-insurance policy. Farther down were the agreement papers for the family trust. Under both of those, an official-looking envelope that Cassie had never seen before held Brad's will.

She sifted through the documents, her dismay growing by the moment. In a short time, she came to a heart-stopping discovery: Brad had put his insurance in his mother's name!

Not only that, but the trust fund that they all four lived on after Brad's salary as a university professor ran out every month was in the children's names with his mother as the trustee.

The only money Cassie could call her own was the miserable balance in their joint checking account, which wouldn't last until the end of the month, and one battered station wagon. There was mortgage life insurance that would pay for the house. But if she read things right, the house would go jointly into her name and Dierdre's.

She wouldn't even own the roof over their heads!

So now it would be Dierdre that planned the funeral, Dierdre with her lofty expression that was the exact image of Brad's. And it would be Dierdre, who had never approved of her in the first place, who would make the decisions on how Cassie and her children lived.

"What kind of hate prompted you to do this to me?" she asked Brad, knowing that only the empty air in the cramped little room at the bank heard her anguished words.

She felt so incredibly lonely and bereft. It seemed that even God had turned his back on her. Why else would he have allowed this to happen? She once had trusted in God's loving care, but that was before Brad destroyed her ability to trust.

She wept silent and bitter tears. No one cared about what happened to her. No one except two small children that she couldn't begin to provide for.

After a moment, she sat up and drew in a deep breath. She brushed away the limp, pale brown hair hanging in her face and lifted her chin. No matter how she felt, one thing was certain. Dierdre was not going to see her cry. Or beg. She'd get through this some way, and once she had, no one was ever going to see her ask for anything again.

"I will never forgive you," she said, even more softly. "Never, Bradley. Never!"

Then Cassie strode from the tiny room, dry eyed. She would never cry for Brad Neel again.

One

Six years later

"Mrs. Neel? Mrs. Neel?" A chorus of small voices worked their way into Cassie's consciousness. She looked up to remember where she was. Of course. Ms. Logan's second-grade class. Listening to the children's stories.

"Stop there for a moment, Katie." The little girl nodded as Cassie smiled at the upturned faces of the children. "Now, one at a time."

But the babble of voices rose again in chorus. "The office. They called on the loudspeaker. Didn't you hear? About lunch."

Cassie had to laugh, holding up her hand to quiet them. "No, James, I didn't hear. And Melody, I'm pretty sure I know what they wanted. Thank you all for looking after me." She looked back to Katie, still intent on finishing her story. "We'll work on this in a minute, okay? I have to go pay for my lunch."

Katie broke into a grin, lighting up her small, pale face. "Okay. You did it again, huh?"

Cassie nodded. "I did it again." Even the second graders knew that Cassie got so involved in her teaching tasks as a teacher's aide that she lost track of everything else. Including ordering lunch, or paying for it. Fortunately, the office staff knew also, and they took care of her, tracking her down and making sure she ordered lunch on the days she ate in the cafeteria.

In the office, Cassie scrounged around in the pocket of her red cardigan. September had stayed warm and turned into October before she'd needed to dig the sweater out of the closet. Whatever was in the pockets was last spring's leftovers. There *had* to be another nickel in among the shredded tissues, cough drop wrappers, and jangling keys.

Her searching fingers passed over the cool metal of a paper clip and pushed away the stub of a pencil. "Gotcha!" she told the elusive silvery disk. "$1.80!" she said with a triumphant smile, adding to the little pile of change on the counter in front of Sandy, the secretary. "Put me down for lunch number two. That's the grilled cheese, right?"

Sandy nodded. Her glasses slid to the end of her nose again, giving her the look of someone's slightly harried mother. Which, as school secretary, she was, eight hours a day, to over six hundred kids. "Are you eating with Zach or Sarah today?"

"Zach. It's his turn." It was part of the routine. Once a week Cassie ate with one of her kids in the school cafeteria instead of brown bagging in the peace and quiet of the faculty lounge. It was much calmer with the adults, but she learned more in the one day she ate with the kids.

Zachary's third-grade class talked about who had lost teeth and compared the merits of various cartoons and video games. Sarah's fifth-grade classmates talked about clothes and music and sometimes even boys. Regarding the latter, Cassie thought they were too young, but she didn't often offer her opinion at the lunch table. No sense being thought of as more of a fossil than she already felt.

Sarah was growing up so fast. She had pointed out this

morning that her shoes were getting too snug again. Cassie knew that last year's jacket wasn't going to make it either. And of course, it was pink and purple, negating the possibility of handing it down to Zach. At eleven her daughter wanted to dress with a feminine flair, not worry about passing down clothing to her kid brother.

Adding all the expenses in her head tired Cassie out. Even if she planned for Christmas to be the usual assortment of needed clothing and a couple books, it wasn't going to let her scrape by under budget. There was no way around it, she was going to have to take another check from Dierdre.

Depending on Brad's mother for money this long after his death disheartened Cassie. Still, she didn't have a choice. There had been no way around the provisions of Brad's will, making his mother executor of his estate and leaving her the trustee who doled out the money to Cassie, the grateful beneficiary. Except she rarely felt grateful. Normally, she just resented Dierdre's control over her finances. Dierdre seemed to positively gloat any time Cassie needed funds.

Sandy broke into her thoughts. "Zach, huh? Well, I'll try to call down and remind you at 11:15."

"Do that. I don't want to be late. But for now I have to go back to Ms. Logan's room. Katie is telling me the most wonderful story about a bear who can read and write."

"Unlike Katie," Sandy said ruefully.

"She's making wonderful progress," Cassie said, eager to defend one of her small charges.

"I'm sure she is. All those kids you work with make wonderful progress, Cassie. You really ought to think about going back and getting that degree. Just think how much more you could help them with your own classroom."

Cassie looked at Sandy with what she knew was a rueful expression. "That's going to have to wait." Like permanently, she added silently, but not to sweet, optimistic Sandy. "Before that I've got two kids who grow out of their clothes at every opportunity and will be in college before we know it."

Zach and Sarah would go to college and finish. That was the one thing she and Dierdre agreed upon. There was precious little else. Cassie headed back to Ms. Logan's room to sit with Katie while she dictated her story to her. When they were done with the words, Cassie would type it into the computer and "publish" the story, leaving room for Katie's illustrations. It would be a wonderful story, she promised the child. Seeing her eyes shine, Cassie could tell that they both believed it.

Leaving Ms. Logan's classroom, she picked up the key to her room and headed down the hall. Some room, she thought as she opened the door. The plaque that said "Mrs. Neel" above the door had replaced one that said "Book Closet." At least she had her own desk and a room. It wasn't as nice as the teachers' desks in their large, airy rooms full of students and windows. But two years of a liberal arts degree didn't really ready her for any kind of job.

When she had married at twenty she convinced herself that it didn't matter if she didn't finish school. She was madly in love with a fascinating professor, and he'd said that as long as he was taking care of her, she didn't need to finish that degree.

Then Brad had insisted on her doing nothing but staying home to be a faculty wife. Before he came into her life, Cassie always figured she herself would be teaching once she finished school. Or working somewhere glamorous, like a publishing company working on textbooks. The babies came in quick succession, and any dreams she had of finishing her degree went straight out the window in a flurry of sweet-smelling baby powder.

It was ironic that all the reasons Brad had given for leaving had been ones he'd created himself, Cassie thought, surveying her little kingdom. She was too narrow, too boring because she stayed at home with the children. The darling little graduate student he'd already picked out to be the second Mrs. Neel before he'd let the first one know she was history, was much brighter. And much younger.

If her image as a housewife and mother had bored Brad, he would have turned to stone by now if he'd been alive, Cassie decided. The most exciting thing in her entire cubbyhole was a row of crayon drawings and a large poster of a window with frilly curtains. If they didn't provide her with the real thing, she could at least remind herself what the outside world looked like with her pretend window.

Some days it felt like that window taped on her wall was all she saw of the outside world. When she wasn't at school, she still had two grade-schoolers and precious little money. Never enough to do the things some of their friends did, like take dance and violin lessons after school. And definitely not enough to pay for child care and tuition if she went back to school herself.

Still, she enjoyed the challenge and reward of helping kids learn. Most of the time that was enough to keep her busy and to stop her yearning for something else. There were times, though, when Cassie knew that there was so much more out there. It just always felt beyond her grasp.

A long time ago, God had been an important part of her life, and she'd looked to him for guidance and love. Since Brad's betrayal, that was all gone. Thanks to Brad, the place in her heart that had been filled with Christ's love was filled with bitterness, disappointment, and hurt. So often she longed to go back to the simple way things were before, when she believed and trusted in God. But that felt as far away, and just as unreachable, as her other dreams.

Outside in the hall a bell rang, pulling Cassie back to the

present. Normally she kept her dark thoughts about the past at bay, and now, turning to the routine of the day, she forced them from her mind. Cassie opened her plan book. Tuesday. That meant fourth-grade reading groups next, third-grade multiplication drills in the afternoon, and lunch with Zach in the middle. She started going through the pile of books on the shelf, looking for the fourth-grade reader.

True to form, Sandy's voice over the loudspeaker surprised Cassie in her fourth-grade classroom. "Please remind Mrs. Neel it's time for her lunch break," came the cheery voice. Twenty small voices joined the teacher in promising to give the reminder. There were some giggles, making Cassie smile as she finished the reading lesson with four children, all of them parked on carpet squares in the corner of the room. It seemed every child in the school knew how much she lost herself in teaching.

There was a chorus of good-byes as she got up and got ready to head down the hall to the cafeteria. She detoured by her cubbyhole to put away the reader, then hurried down to the open doors where the third graders were coming in from before-lunch recess. Zach was there, a breeze catching his jacket and blowing it back (it wasn't zipped, as usual) to reveal his lanky frame. His blond hair, just long enough to curl, framed his sweet face.

He was such a good kid. They both were, Cassie told herself as her son came through the door, stopped at the handwashing station, and got ready to go to lunch with her. She reminded herself once again of how lucky she was to have two wonderful children.

Zach seemed in more of a hurry than usual to get to the lunchroom. Cassie raised an eyebrow and cocked her head in question, keeping to the silence rules in the hall outside the fifth-grade classrooms with their open doors while still asking the question. "Officer Winter's eating lunch with us," Zach whispered. "I want to get us a seat at his table."

Officer Winter? Who was he? Cassie wondered. Someone important if Zach's hurry to get to lunch was any indication. The name felt familiar, but not in a way she could put a finger on. Shrugging off her speculation, Cassie fell in line behind her son to get milk, a tray and silverware, and a golden grilled-cheese sandwich. Zach zoomed ahead of her, coasting by the food bar just long enough to get a handful of raw veggie sticks and a cookie from the smiling cafeteria worker before scooting on to the table at the far edge of the room.

He slid in beside a man Cassie assumed was Officer Winter. Even sitting down, the officer towered over the third graders. His crisp tan uniform was emblazoned with all sorts of badges and patches, and there was obviously a real gun in that leather holster at his side.

Tan and brown. That was Cassie's initial impression of the man, not just the uniform. Tan skin, smooth and glowing. Glossy dark brown hair, shorter than Zach's but still with a little wave to it. He seemed to be taking a moment of quiet before he ate, an oasis of calm in the sea of chaos that was the normal state of the lunchroom. When he looked up and saw Cassie, he tried to stand, a neat trick when wedged between the long, narrow table and its small backless bench with third graders crowding around him.

"No, please," Cassie said, motioning for him to stay seated. "Really, it's all right."

"Okay." He had bright blue eyes, breaking her impression of all the brown. And a ready smile that stretched a mobile mouth, making his eyes crinkle a little in the corners. He was so surprisingly good looking that Cassie had to concentrate on setting her tray down gently and sliding onto the facing bench. The officer sat down again and extended a hand.

"I'm Lee Winter. The DARE officer assigned to Dogwood." Cassie shook his proffered hand as soon as hers were free. His handshake was brief but incredibly warm. And somewhere in it, she discovered why Lee Winter's name had sounded familiar.

"You quit the Highway Patrol?" she blurted out, watching his flash of confusion with a little shock of pain.

"Have we met?" he asked. "You seem to know me."

She sat down all the way on the bench, wondering how to answer. "I'm Cassie Neel, Zach's mother. And also an education aide here. We met, briefly. About six years ago. You came to my door."

"I remember now," Lee said. The briefest flicker of recognition warmed his expression. "Nights like that were the reason I came over here from the patrol. I'm sorry."

"Don't be," Cassie told him. "I have a very nice life now." She surprised herself by meaning every word of what she said.

"Okay. Well, nice to meet you. Again." He seemed to mean it, too. Cassie was struck by the open, friendly manner he used. Lee Winter obviously liked his job as a liaison between the school and the police department. He appeared to be comfortable surrounded by little kids, and they obviously thought the world of him. Zach wasn't the only child who hurried to the table to sit with Officer Winter.

"How's the program going this year?" Cassie asked. She had been at the school long enough to know the schedule for the Drug Abuse Resistance Education program, which the kids all called DARE. Officer Winter would spend a couple days a week for most of the year in the fifth-grade classrooms, talking about ways to avoid drugs and alcohol. And he'd drop in to the younger children's rooms as well, doing a presentation with one room or another so that he was a constant presence for them.

She wondered how she'd missed seeing him before this. He'd replaced another officer in the DARE program at the beginning of the school year. But how had she missed running into him until now?

He'd just taken a bite of sandwich when she asked her question, so it was a moment before he answered. "Fine. They're great kids, as usual. Cassie Neel, hmm? Have you got one in fifth grade here as well?"

Cassie nodded, impressed. There had to be nearly a hundred fifth graders, and after only a few weeks this man could pick out a single name. "Sarah. She's in Ms. Scott's room."

The officer smiled, pleased with his ability. "Yeah. I think she's the one that got me in the dodgeball game yesterday during gym."

Cassie chuckled. "Now, that takes courage."

He flashed her a marvelous grin. "You're right," he answered. "But if I'm supposed to promote this idea that healthy bodies are a great thing and that they need to take care of theirs, they better see me doing the same thing."

"I think that's about as brave as anything else you'd have to do as a police officer." Cassie was surprised. She was almost flirting with a near stranger. At the least she was talking very easily with a man she'd only known ten minutes, if you didn't count that horrible half hour six years before. It wasn't like her. She didn't usually have time for men, and she certainly didn't want one in her life. There was enough complication there already without adding a man, no matter how attractive.

Besides, she told herself, looking down at her plate, Zach had made it clear that Lee Winter was the children's hero, someone to talk to themselves. So, though Cassie didn't ignore the handsome police officer during lunch, she let the children around them enjoy his undivided attention.

Surprisingly, Zach didn't say much. And he had this funny look, as if he were planning something particularly Zachlike. Cassie was thankful when lunch was over and he hadn't done anything to embarrass her in public. She and Lee Winter stood at about the same time, and he told her how nice it was to have met her. Of course she'd see him again. In a school where both of them spent their time, she'd run into him dozens of times now that she knew who he was.

"Mom? Bye. See you later, okay?" Zach was ready to join the line to return to his classroom.

"Okay, sport." She resisted the temptation to ruffle his hair, reminding herself that at his age, he might see that as an affront. Motherly affection was to be reserved for closed cars and such, not open cafeterias.

"Mom?" Zach was still there, bright eyes looking up at her. "Did you like having lunch with Officer Winter?"

"Sure, Zach. He seems nice."

"He's great!" Zach said enthusiastically. Then his teacher started the line moving, and Cassie's thoughts started moving on to her afternoon classroom assignments, never for a moment wondering what Zach's question might mean.

Lee Winter stood outside Dogwood Elementary School, gazing at the building. He had so many things to do this afternoon. There were reports to finish in his tiny cubicle back at the station. He had DARE workbooks to look at for nearly one hundred kids. He had a two hour parents' program to plan. Now why, instead of doing any of this, did he want to go back into the school and track down Cassie Neel and follow her around like a puppy?

He could still smell the faint scent of her perfume, like springtime in the woods. Even more compelling had been the look in her eyes, that incredible burden she seemed to be bearing. Was it his imagination, or had it lifted a little, for just a moment, while she ate lunch with her son and the rest of the noisy, obstreperous third grade? Cassie seemed to thrive on the company of children. He couldn't help wondering how she felt about his company, although Lee told himself it was wishful thinking on his part that she might think of him at all.

It was good to see her again. With most people he dealt with as a police officer, he never knew the outcome of their stories. For the offenders he arrested there was often a court date and a sentencing, but past that, everything was a mystery. How many went straight? Gained their parole only to do, again, whatever had sent them to prison in the first place? How many accident victims picked up the pieces of their shattered lives, or those of their loved ones, triumphing over their tragedies? He never knew. The not knowing was something he'd learned to put in God's hands a long time ago.

That was why today felt so right, so good. It was as though God had handed him back a gift. Cassie Neel was no longer the frightened young widow to whom he'd delivered the devastating news of her husband's death on that rainy night so many years ago.

Instead, she had blossomed into someone independent and happy in her work. She seemed to relish being with her kids, and other kids, every day. *Thank you, Father,* Lee prayed. *It's always good to see that sometimes things turn out okay after all.*

Even as he said his brief prayer, Lee felt a nagging sensation that not everything was all right in Cassie's life. There was something in her expression, her eyes, but he couldn't pinpoint what it was, or even why he had noticed it. He also had to wonder why God had brought her into his life.

So where do I fit into all this, Lord? he found himself asking. *I hope I do fit in someplace, because I enjoyed seeing her again.*

Face it, Winter, he told himself on the way to the black van painted with DARE program slogans. *You more than enjoyed it. You can't wait to see Cassie Neel again.* He got out his keys and let out a deep sigh as he opened the driver's side door.

No matter how wonderful it was to think about Cassie, it

was time to get back to the work at hand. He swung in behind the wheel, thinking that like the fifth grade boys he spent so much time with today, he would rather stare out a classroom window and daydream than go back to work after lunch.

And there was no one more perfect to daydream about than the lovely young widow, Cassie Neel.

Two

Cassie sat staring at the telephone. She always did this when it was time to call Dierdre. She disliked calling so much that she put it off for days, arguing with herself the whole time, rehearsing the call in her head. Of course, it never went the way she planned. Dierdre always got in some little dig or another and seemed to gloat over the fact that Cassie was asking her for money again.

It didn't matter that the terms of Brad's will had been very specific: All the interest from the trust fund was to be spent on the children as the checks were disbursed quarterly. But as trustee, Dierdre never put a check in an envelope and simply mailed it to Cassie. Instead, Cassie had to get on the phone and hem and haw and hint until she came right out and asked for the money. Dierdre never seemed to tire of their little cat-and-mouse game.

The children didn't realize how hard earned their possessions were. Sarah, especially, was at an age where she was beginning to notice just what her friends had and she didn't. How her clothes came from the discount store if her mother bought them, and the higher priced clothing with the "right" labels came only from Grandma. She was always bubbling over about their shopping trips when she came home from spending a weekend with Dierdre. Cassie couldn't bear to break it to the child that the money her grandmother lavished on her was hers to begin with. Even though she felt it wasn't right, she wasn't going to be the one to point that out to her daughter.

Zach was still oblivious to clothes and music and the pricier things in life, except for sports equipment. Brad had never been very athletic, so as a result, Dierdre's house in Kansas City lacked things to keep Cassie's active son entertained when the children visited. More than once he'd come home from a trip with a new leather soccer ball or a bat and glove. And of course, that made his grandmother a wonderful person in his eyes.

So Cassie waited to make the phone calls she dreaded. Waited and stewed, doing her chores when the children came home from school with her, rehearsed her speeches under her breath while she made dinner. Then there was homework to supervise, and baths, and tucking Zach in. Sarah stayed up later, tape player playing softly in her room with the door shut while she read.

Only when it was quiet in the hallway, with no light peeking from under her daughter's door, did Cassie start her serious staring at the phone. Even then, she let it taunt her as she twisted a lock of her pale brown hair as she worked up the courage to dial Dierdre's number.

When Cassie called, Dierdre never let the machine pick up the message. It was as if the older woman knew in advance just how long it would take Cassie to make that call, because she was always home to receive it. This time was no different.

It had been dark for hours, daylight savings time having ended a week before. The darkness of winter was closing in, and Cassie was reminded again that the children couldn't have winter coats until she dialed the phone. Her paycheck only went so far, and a hundred dollars worth of warm jackets weren't in her slender budget.

So there was good reason to call Dierdre. Why had she put it off? As the phone was ringing, she knew the answer to that question. Knew it as soon as Dierdre answered. "Hello?"

"Hello? Dierdre?"

"Cassie." The expectant tone in the older woman's voice had flattened in two syllables. "I thought it might be you." *But I was hoping it wouldn't be, for a change,* Cassie added silently, knowing what her mother-in-law was probably thinking. "How are the children?"

"Fine. You should see how Sarah is growing."

"You're not making her wear last year's shoes again, are you?" Her tone was sharp, almost accusatory.

Cassie was immediately on the defensive. How did Dierdre manage this? With the rest of the world Cassie could be strong, decisive, in control. With Dierdre she felt like a recalcitrant child. "Of course not," she told her. "But even those I bought before school started aren't going to last much longer. Her feet are only half a size smaller than mine."

"Well, we knew she wasn't going to be petite." There was almost a sniff in her voice. Cassie felt her hand tightening on the telephone receiver in frustration. Leave it to Dierdre to aggravate her in less than a minute. "And Zachary?"

Why did her son's name always sound outlandish when Dierdre said it? Cassie knew that her mother-in-law had wanted to name him Bradley Jonathan Neel II. The fact that they'd actually used Jonathan for his middle name placated her not at all. Cassie loved her son's name, except when Dierdre said it. Then it sounded like something that crawled out from under a rock.

"Zach's fine too. He's the fastest boy in his class in the six-hundred-yard dash."

31

"How's his reading? You *are* making him read, aren't you, not just letting him doodle around outside."

"Of course. I think right now he's working on *The Mouse and the Motorcycle,*" Cassie said.

This time Dierdre's sniff was audible. "When he was that age, Bradley was already reading real literature, like Rudyard Kipling and Sir Walter Scott."

And sneaking comic books every chance he got, Cassie said to herself. "Zach's teacher is perfectly happy with what he's learning."

"Of course. He goes to a public school," Dierdre countered, her emphasis on *public,* as in mediocre. "If you'd only listened to my suggestions about coming back here and letting them go to Oakbrook as Bradley did. I still would like to—"

"Really, Dierdre, I don't want to get into this again," Cassie interrupted, as gently as she possibly could. "I'm sure it's a lovely idea, but the children are so happy here. It's their home. And honestly, their grade school is ranked very high among the elementary schools in the area, public or private."

The silence was pointed. "Yes, well, I'm sure," Dierdre finally said, her tone extremely stiff. "But I'm sure you didn't call to discuss the state of elementary education."

"Actually, I didn't," Cassie admitted. *Just once it would be so nice if she would ask if the children needed money. Or better, just mailed the check without being asked.* But the mailbox had been empty of anything but bills and advertising flyers for a week. And the silence ticked on from Dierdre's end of the telephone until Cassie took a deep breath. No more small talk.

"I called about the children's winter coats. They've both outgrown them, and it's getting colder. I really need that interest check before I can buy them new coats, Dierdre."

There, it was out. Now a new tone would creep into the older woman's voice. Almost jubilant. She'd heard the admission again that Cassie was a lousy money manager, and that only her kind and constant help kept her family's heads above water. Right on schedule, Cassie could hear the smile in Dierdre's voice.

"Of course, I'll be more than happy to send it. I can't imagine how it slipped my mind. Had I realized that you *needed* it so urgently, I would have just sent it when the quarterly statement came."

"Of course," Cassie murmured. It wasn't what she wanted to say. In fact, her jaw hurt from clenching it to keep from saying what she would have liked. Once the conversation was over, she would head to her bedroom and strangle her bed pillow. Those poor defenseless feathers inside never had a chance after a call to Dierdre.

"I suppose I could just take them shopping when they come up next month to visit," Dierdre said. "They are coming, aren't they?"

"Of course they are. I'll meet you in Columbia at the mall, the same as usual." It had been their arrangement for years. Dierdre claimed it was to keep Cassie from having to put much mileage on her car driving all the way to Kansas City. Cassie suspected it was so Dierdre could have just a few more hours with her grandchildren under her control. "But really, I'd rather get their coats myself. And there's always a few other things they need."

"I'm sure. Zachary is so active he's probably terribly hard on his clothes." *If you could just get him to sit still for a while...* Cassie could hear the unspoken hints the older woman was giving her.

For once she decided not to rise to the bait. "He certainly is," she said cheerfully. "And I have to go work on fifth grade science papers. So if you'll excuse me, I'll let you go. I'll look for that check, Dierdre."

"I'm sure you will," came the dry reply before the dial tone. Cassie hung up the phone and leaned against the sofa in relief. She'd survived again. Another round with the dragon and she still had all her skin.

Before she knew it, Wednesday had rolled around again, and she was digging change out of her pocket so she could eat lunch with Zach again. Sarah's turn had passed uneventfully, with no food disasters by any of her tablemates or jokes so gross that they put Cassie off her lunch. As the kids got older, that counted as a successful lunch experience in the school lunchroom.

Zach had seemed unusually anxious to have her remember lunch with him today. Cassie thought it was sweet. She knew that it wouldn't be much longer before she'd lose this experience. Next year Sarah would be in middle school, where most kids didn't even acknowledge having parents, much less want to eat lunch with them. And Zach would be taller, ganglier, on his way to adolescence.

For now it was nice to have a curly-haired innocent who wanted to eat lunch with her. Cassie found her change, deposited it in the office, and ordered a grilled chicken sandwich. Going back to her cubicle, she picked up reading books for several different groups and lost herself in the daily routine until the intercom squawked at 11:30, drawing her out of her busy day.

The doors to the playground let in a rush of cold air. Cassie was glad the check from Dierdre had come without further ado, and she had gotten both the kids coats before this cold snap. Zach looked great in his navy and red jacket. Of course he didn't have the hood up as he came into the building, but that was probably too much to expect.

He washed his hands quickly and deposited his paper towel

in the waiting wastebasket. "Hi, Mom. Let's go. I don't want to be late."

There was such a purposeful bounce to his stride. If today had been pizza day, Cassie could understand his speed, but Zach had never before been in this much of a hurry for grilled chicken. There wasn't even ice cream for dessert. Cassie briefly wondered what was going on.

She found out once they got to the cafeteria. Zach handed his lunch ticket to the smiling worker behind the computer terminal, who swiped it through the scanner while he got them both chocolate milk. "Officer Winter's going to sit with us again," Zach said, in the offhand, casual tone he usually saved for progress reports and broken windows.

"Oh? How did you manage that?" Cassie asked. She knew that none of the classes would get the company of the DARE officer for lunch twice in two weeks by chance. There were just too many classrooms and too little time for repeats that close together.

Zach shrugged elaborately and pushed his tray through the line. It was almost funny to watch him in front of her, craning his neck to make sure the tall figure was at the right lunch table.

Zach must really be distracted, Cassie told herself when she watched him take a full serving of salad, one of the basic green food groups he never touched at home. Perhaps he wanted to impress the police officer with his healthy eating habits. Cassie wondered how impressed he'd be with hers—cheese on the grilled chicken sandwich, dressing on her salad, and a frozen fruit bar for dessert.

If he didn't like it, he could just blame her metabolism, Cassie told herself, putting a little three bean salad in the one empty compartment in her tray. Even with eating in the school cafeteria with the kids as often as she did, her figure still tended to be on the thin side. Other women her age bemoaned the battle of the bulge. Cassie couldn't ever remember having any bulges to battle with, except during two pregnancies, and even then the extra weight had seemed to be all baby.

When they got to the table, Cassie wondered how much of the third grade was in on this little scheme. There were no seats at the table except the two end places next to Lee Winter. Every other single spot was filled by a nonchalant-looking kid. And of course, Zach insisted that his mother should slide onto the bench first.

Cassie knew there was no way to demur without causing a scene. And sitting next to a handsome man for one lunch period wasn't exactly torture. So she smiled weakly when Lee looked up from his tray, then she slid onto the hard bench.

The smile she got back was dazzling. It made Cassie sit down a little harder than she'd intended. His eyes were really as incredibly blue as she'd imagined. And his manner just as easy with all these wonderful, noisy, obstreperous kids. "Hey there," he said, smiling again. "I hoped you were going to make it today."

"Yes, well, I guess I did." *Real intelligent conversation.* Cassie paid attention to her salad for a moment or two, willing herself not to dribble dressing down her oxford cloth shirt. At least she'd worn the cute vest with the turkeys on it.

"Hey, Officer Winter," Zach piped up. "I was wondering if I could ask you something."

"Sure, Zach. Ask away." Lee Winter had beautiful hands for a man. Cassie could see them next to her when she looked down at her lunch tray and enjoyed the long, slender fingers and the sprinkle of brown-gold hair there. No rings or jewelry to distract her, except for a plain watch in a brushed silver finish.

"It's my mom's birthday next week and me an' Sarah want to

get her something really cool. If we paid, would you take her out to dinner?"

Cassie's surprise was so great that her carefully balanced forkful of salad slid into her lap. It was a moment before she could say anything. When she did, the words were clipped and precise. "Zachary Jonathan Neel, you are grounded. For life."

Three

There was as much silence around them following Cassie's pronouncement as she could expect in the crowded cafeteria. Zach, of course, looked stunned. "But Mom, I thought you'd like it. Officer Winter is really cool. And he didn't say no, did he?"

Cassie looked over at the handsome policeman. "Zach, that just isn't how things are done. I'm sorry, Officer Winter, really. I've been a widow since Zach was a toddler, and I don't date much, and I guess he just doesn't know how it's done."

Cassie was still flushed with embarrassment from her son's proposal, and Lee Winter's answering smile left her breathless as well. "You mean it's supposed to work differently from this?" he asked. "I have kids try to fix me up with their moms all the time. I do have to admit this is the first time I've been offered as a birthday gift, though."

His laugh warmed Cassie more than the blush that was fading as she looked at Zach. His eyes were filling with tears. "Honest, Mom, I thought you'd like it. Sarah's gonna pound me for messing up."

"No, Sarah is not going to pound you, young man, not for

this or anything else. And it was sweet of you to think of such a nice treat for my birthday."

"So it's not me you're objecting to?" Lee put in, raising a brow. "You were so quick to answer, I figured you didn't want to go out with me."

It took a moment for Cassie to find her tongue. "No, really, it's not that at all. It's just that, well, I haven't been out on a date in over a decade. And I couldn't expect anybody to take me anyplace based on an eight-year-old's invitation."

She was staring at the table again, trying to collect her thoughts. From her vantage point of the scarred tabletop, she could see Lee's hand slide over and cover hers. His hand was incredibly warm and welcoming on top of hers. She felt little shock waves from his touch, waking long-dormant feelings inside her. His hand stayed on hers only a moment, then he pulled it away.

"It happens all the time to me, you know," he said softly. She almost had to strain to hear him in the din of the cafeteria. "I go all kinds of places on the invitation of eight-year-olds. It's how I gain their trust. That's pretty important when you're trying to shape the rest of their lives. And I'd like to take you out, for your birthday or any other day, Cassie. What do you say?"

For a moment she couldn't say anything. It was as if her ordered life had turned upside down in a heartbeat. Ten minutes ago her biggest worry was getting through lunch without spilling salad dressing on her turkey vest. Now she had an intriguing, handsome gentleman asking to take her out for her birthday.

She sighed deeply. "I can't do this, Officer Winter, really."

"Why not?" His blue eyes flashed a challenge. "I'd like to take you out. Zach and Sarah want to give you a treat for your birthday. You want to disappoint two little kids and a cop?"

Cassie had to smile. "I guess when you put it that way, it would be a terrible thing to say no, wouldn't it?" She felt a giddy rush of feelings bubbling inside her.

"It would." He was trying to look solemn, Cassie could tell. It wasn't working very well. There was still a sparkle to those blue eyes, and a smile was tugging at the corner of his mouth.

"Then I guess I had better say yes."

The smile won. "Great," Lee said. "Can I have your phone number so that I can call you after work and set things up?"

"Sure. Let me write it down for you," Cassie said, reaching for her purse. That was no mean feat in the crowded space, but amazingly she managed to get the purse she'd stowed under the bench, find a scrap of paper and a pen, and write down her number for Lee. He took it, flashing her another smile.

"Thanks. I'll call once I get off my shift, and we'll set things up." He reached over Cassie and ruffled Zach's curls. "Now don't make this a habit, understand, Zach. I don't do this for just anybody. And I wouldn't want the other kids thinking I'm running a mom escort service, okay?"

Zach's eyes were huge. "Sure, Officer Winter. Thanks. I won't tell anybody if you don't want me to."

Lee nodded. "This is our secret." He looked around at the other third graders surrounding them at the crowded table. "A secret we're *all* going to keep, right gang? I know we talk in class about secrets to keep and secrets not to keep. Please tell me you understand which kind this is."

A short girl with freckles giggled from across the table. "We won't tell, Officer Winter," she said, then covered her mouth to stifle more giggles. "But, can we come to the wedding?"

That one left even Lee speechless. Cassie had to laugh. He didn't have a clue what he was in for. "Come on, Kelsey. You know that grown-ups don't get married after one date. We're going out for a burger or something. Not getting married."

Kelsey dissolved in giggles again. "Okay, Mrs. Neel. If you say so."

She looked at Lee Winter, feeling sympathy for him. "You can still change your mind."

"No way. I said I'd take you out for your birthday, and I intend to do it. But we're not getting married, Kelsey. I mean, I don't even *kiss* on the first date."

That left Kelsey helpless with giggles. And Cassie feeling flushed again and very thankful for the whistle that suddenly sounded, signaling two minutes of silence for everybody to finish their lunches. She didn't finish her chicken sandwich in two minutes, but at least she had a respite from having to look into Lee Winter's teasing blue eyes again.

"Are you sure I look all right?" Cassie asked Sarah while she brushed her hair again. It just wouldn't behave tonight of all nights.

"Mom, yes, really," Sarah said, sounding exasperated. "You look fine."

Cassie glanced in the mirror again. Other than her flyaway hair, everything looked okay. The soft flowered rayon dress was one of the two outfits she had that she deemed too nice for school. She hadn't smeared the little bit of makeup she'd put on, even though her hands trembled with nervous energy and excitement.

A date. What did people talk about on dates? Feeling panic rising, Cassie cast about trying to think of somebody to call and ask. But most of her friends were either married or single moms like herself, too busy, broke, and tired to worry about such things.

"Hey, Sarah?" Her voice sounded a little shaky, Cassie thought. "I've got something to ask you."

Sarah, looking very tall and self-confident as she stood next to Cassie, assumed it was about her duties for the evening. "I promise we'll be okay. You've let me watch Zach before when you've gone grocery shopping. And yes, I've got those three different numbers for the neighbors. Really, we'll be all right."

"I know you will, sweetie. I'm sure you'll do just fine." The baby-sitting course at the library that Sarah had taken a few weeks earlier had reinforced everything that Cassie had been teaching her for months. The kids felt like the least of her worries right now. "But that's not what I was going to ask you about...."

Sarah wrinkled her nose and stepped back from the mirror, looking wise. "Well, you look okay. And you smell *great*. Aren't you glad I still had some of that perfume left that Grandma gave me?"

"I *am* glad." Cassie said it like she meant it, which she did. It touched her that Sarah wanted to share her perfume with her mother. Dierdre would probably do a slow boil if she knew, but chances of that were slim. "But that wasn't what I was going to ask you. When Officer Winter comes to your classroom, what do you talk about? Besides DARE, I mean? What does he like to do?"

Sarah's forehead creased in concentration. "I don't know. Mostly we just talk about drug education. How it's stupid to drink and drive or take somebody else's prescriptions. Stuff like that." She paused in thought for a minute. "He likes animals. I know, because he saw the endangered animal posters we made for science, he knew more about them than the teacher did."

Animals. It was a start, anyway. She nodded. "Okay, sweetie. Thanks."

"Sure." Sarah's look seemed puzzled and amused at the same time. "Mom, are you nervous?"

Cassie's laugh gave her away. "Sure am. I'll be honest, Sarah. I haven't gone out on a date since I was nineteen."

"And you were going out with daddy?"

"Right. So I'm not real sure of how these things go anymore."

"Oh, Mom, you'll do fine," Sarah said, patting her on the shoulder. The ringing of the doorbell forestalled any other conversation.

Cassie found herself nearly leaping to answer the door. "Relax, Mom," Sarah said, sounding much older than eleven. "You'll be fine."

Cassie hoped fervently that her daughter was right. She slowed down to cross the remainder of the hall and the living room. Peeking out the side window next to the door, she could make out a tall figure.

She opened the door. Lee stood there, looking much more composed than she felt. "Hi, Lee. Come in for a minute, won't you?"

"Sure," he said, stepping into the room. He looked at Cassie, and even though it was simply a warm, friendly look, she got little shivers returning his gaze. After a moment, he glanced across the room. "Hi, Sarah," he said, waving. "Where's Zach?"

"Probably in his room," Sarah said. "He said there was too much girl stuff going on for him, so he went in there to hide."

Lee laughed. "I see. Well, you can go tell him it's safe to come out now," Lee said, winking at Cassie. Just that small gesture sent another thrill of delight coursing through her. He extended a hand in her direction. "Happy birthday."

"Thank you," Cassie said, taking his hand. It was warm and dry. She hoped her palm wasn't as damp as she thought it was. How could she get this nervous over a simple dinner? It wasn't going to be anything formal. It wouldn't even last that long. And if she made a complete and utter fool of herself, she'd never have to see Lee again, at least not socially. Telling herself all this didn't help much. She still felt shakier than she had since the senior prom.

Lee seemed to sense her nervousness and gave her another warm smile that made the skin around his deep blue eyes crinkle. Cassie discovered she liked that look immensely. "It would be nice if I could project this image of a man about town, but it's been quite a while since I've dated, too." He shrugged and grinned. "I've really been looking forward to this evening."

She was touched that he remembered what she said about not dating for over a decade and was already set to put her at ease. Before she could respond, Zach thundered into the room. "Hey, Officer Winter. How's it going? I guess you want this." He was waving a handful of dollar bills. "Where you going to take Mom, anyway?"

"I figured we'd go to Shoney's," Lee said. He took the proffered money. "Thanks for the funds. Next time, I'm taking you guys out someplace to make up for this, okay?"

Cassie's heart swelled watching her son with the police officer. She was so glad that Lee was treating him seriously and not patting him on the head and refusing his money.

Lee looked grand standing in her living room. His dark pants and twill sports shirt were as sharply pressed as his uniform had been and fit him just as well. However, it was who he was inside, especially his respect for her children, that impressed Cassie the most.

She must have lost herself in thought for a moment because she realized that they were all looking at her expectantly. "I'm sorry. Did you ask me something?"

Lee nodded. "Are you ready to go?"

"Sure. Let me get my coat," Cassie said, grabbing her purse off a nearby chair and heading to the closet.

"You'll need it. I'm afraid my personal transportation isn't as snug as a squad car," Lee said, sounding apologetic.

"Whatever it is, it will be fine," Cassie assured him. She gave Sarah last minute instructions and went to the door, where Lee still stood waiting. "I'm ready."

He opened the door for her and ushered her out. "Make sure to lock this behind us," he called to Sarah, then stood on the front porch until he heard her do just that. "Great," he said. "It's good to know she's a careful sitter."

"This is her first time watching Zach in the evening," Cassie said. "She says some of her classmates have been watching brothers and sisters for years. But I guess I'm a little cautious about things like that."

"Suits me just fine," Lee said, holding out his hand. "As long as you're not too cautious to ride in a Jeep without the windows. I know it's getting a little nippy, but I haven't had the time to put them back in since the last warm spell."

He held the door open when they got to the vehicle. Cassie gracefully boosted herself onto the high seat. "Cautious about this?" she teased as she settled back. "Fresh air on a starry night? I think it's pretty wonderful." *And I was worried about my hair,* she thought to herself, struggling with a joyful laugh that threatened to burst out.

He gave her another marvelous smile. "I think so, too," he said as he climbed in on the driver's side.

Four

The restaurant looked warm and welcoming after the breezy drive in Lee's open Jeep. Cassie felt exhilarated by the November wind, not frozen, when she stepped out onto the pavement. In front of her the restaurant lights twinkled, and Lee held open the entrance door. She felt, suddenly, as if she were embarking on a wonderful adventure.

Inside, the hostess and the server welcomed Lee like a friend. Cassie had no problem making small talk as they ordered, and soon there was a cup of coffee in front of her so she had something to occupy her hands.

"So, how long have you been a DARE officer?" Cassie found herself asking Lee as they waited for their food.

"About four years. This is my third school. It's really my favorite part of the job. I've worked regular street stuff and did a very short stint in Narcotics, but that was even worse than the Highway Patrol as far as I was concerned. For now, this is it, as long as they'll have me."

"Do they rotate you frequently?" Cassie asked, hoping that now that they were becoming friends Lee wouldn't be leaving right away.

"Not usually, unless there's some kind of problem. More than likely, I'll stay at Dogwood for a couple years. I'm probably going to take the sergeant's test when it's offered next, but that shouldn't change my status at the school."

"You seem to be very good at what you do. The kids sure like being with you."

Lee smiled. "I could say the same thing about you. I think Zach's whole class gets excited when you eat lunch with them, not just Zach. You seem to be a pretty popular person around there."

"I like being with them," Cassie admitted. "I wish I had my own classroom, maybe second or third grade, or as a reading specialist. The kids are so much fun, and I love helping them."

"What keeps you from doing it?" Lee said, leaning forward.

"Education. Money. Time. All of the above," Cassie said. "I only have half of my college degree, and it's not in education. It would probably take me about three years, nights and summers, to do it. There's nobody to watch the kids, and I don't have the funds for tuition even if there was somebody to watch them. So…" she held both hands palm upwards and gave him a small shrug. "This is okay for now."

"I hope you find a way to be a teacher, Cassie. You'd be a good one," Lee said.

The waitress with a full tray kept Cassie from having to make a reply. She didn't know what she would have said if the young woman hadn't appeared, balancing hamburgers and setting them on the table in front of her and Lee. Teaching was the desire of her heart, but she knew she wasn't likely to fulfill that dream. By the time the kids were old enough to manage on their own while she went back to school, any spare money would have to be put away for their impending college years. It was far more important that Sarah and Zach complete their degrees so neither of them would ever find themselves in her predicament.

Dierdre would help with their schooling, of course. She valued education too highly to let her grandchildren go without. But she'd never do it all, even if she could afford it. Cassie suspected it was because she got too much pleasure watching Cassie struggle. She tried to push the depressing thoughts away. It was her birthday, and she was out with a fascinating man. Now was not the time to think about Dierdre or wasted dreams.

She glanced at Lee, ready to say something, then noticed he was quiet, eyes closed, paused over his meal. For a moment she couldn't imagine what he was doing, then it dawned on her. In the crowded warmth of the restaurant, her big, tough policeman was saying grace over his food. As if drawn by her gaze, he looked up. "Sorry, I didn't mean to interrupt you," she said, trying not to stammer. "I just didn't expect…"

"That I'd pray in a public place?" He smiled gently. "It takes a little getting used to, but I can't imagine not doing it anymore. Want to join me?"

Cassie felt as if she were stepping out on a limb. A very narrow one that wasn't likely to bear her weight. People would stare. She would feel as uncomfortable as if the kids were along and getting into a burping contest at the table.

But she was with Lee. And he seemed perfectly at ease offering to pray with her in this place. Suddenly she couldn't refuse. "All right," she said quietly. "Yes, please. Go ahead."

He stretched out his hands and took hers. His fingers were so warm and strong. She bowed her head as he began to speak softly.

"Heavenly Father, we thank you for bringing us together in this place. Thank you for Cassie's birthday and give her many more of them, each more wonderful than the last. Bless this food as it nourishes our bodies, and bless our companionship as it nourishes our minds. In Jesus' name, Amen."

"Amen," Cassie found herself whispering. Lee released her hands and reached for the catsup bottle. She looked around quickly. Nobody had noticed their prayer. At least no one was staring. There would be more fuss at the table if the waitresses sang "Happy Birthday." As she glanced across the table for the mustard, she wondered about the sudden warmth that seemed to envelop her. Maybe saying grace in a crowded restaurant wasn't so odd after all.

There were so many questions she wanted to ask him, but suddenly she felt tongue-tied and shy. Whatever she'd imagined people talking about on a first date, this wasn't it. She concentrated on her hamburger for a while, trying to frame the questions spinning in her head.

They did sing "Happy Birthday" to her in the restaurant. Cassie found herself feeling much more embarrassed over being surrounded by singing servers than she felt earlier saying grace with Lee. She wondered what that said about her but couldn't answer that question.

"How's your cake?" Lee asked a little while later. The ice cream was melting a little into a puddle around the chocolate cake.

"It's great, but I promised Zach and Sarah that I'd have cake and ice cream with them when I got home. Would you like to join us?"

"Sure, I'd love to. But I don't want to horn in on a family celebration."

She grinned. "You made my kids' day by agreeing to take me out for my birthday dinner, Lee. I think that practically makes you honorary family," Cassie said, "for tonight."

Lee's answering smile was priceless. "Then why don't we get out of here and go light some candles? How many are we lighting, anyway, Cassie?"

"Too many," she said, raising a brow.

"I guess that isn't a very good question to ask a lady, is it?" Lee said. "My mom would probably clobber me for that one. And Miss Dorothy would skin me alive."

Cassie found herself smiling in spite of herself. "Who's Miss Dorothy?"

"A lady of great taste and refinement who prays for me at church. And lectures me on my deportment. Keeps watch over me, since she knows there's two hundred miles between me and my real grandmother. She considers it her duty to keep me in line. You'd love her."

"I think I would," Cassie said. She'd conjured up a mental picture of Miss Dorothy as he spoke of her in such loving terms. It was intriguing to think of an older lady keeping this strapping young man in line.

"I'll introduce you sometime," Lee said, sounding certain. He paid their bill and escorted Cassie to his waiting vehicle. They drove home in companionable silence until about three blocks from Cassie's house.

Driving up a poorly lit hill, Lee suddenly put on the brakes, hard. It touched Cassie that when he did, he instinctively flung his right arm out to protect his passenger from any forward movement.

"Whoa. I almost didn't see that little fella," Lee said, quickly maneuvering the Jeep to the side of the road. He looked at her, seeming apologetic. "Do you mind if I get out and look? I can't leave the little guy on the side of the road."

"Of course, but I didn't see what we almost hit. What are we looking for?"

"A dog. Maybe a puppy. Hard to see in the dark."

It was Lee who found the animal shivering on the brink of a ditch not too far from where they had pulled over. "Hey there," he said softly. "C'mon, pup, it's okay. Nobody's going to hurt you." He kept crooning softly to the dog until the little animal let himself be picked up.

"Is he all right? I know you didn't hit him."

"No, but I think somebody did. He seems to have a sore front leg. Maybe broken. No tags, either." Still cradling the dog, he looked up at Cassie. "Do you want me to drop you off at home before I take him to the vet? This late at night, it's going to be a run to O'Fallon to the emergency clinic."

Cassie felt a rush of pity for the shivering brown puppy nestled in Lee's arms, looking scared. "I'll go with you. You'll need me to hold him while you drive."

Lee carried the pup until they got to the Jeep. Once Cassie was settled in her seat and buckled in, he handed her the puppy. The little animal yelped in the transfer, and Cassie stroked his smooth head to comfort him. "It's okay, little fella. We'll take care of you." Lee rummaged around in the back of the Jeep and came up with a blanket.

Cassie regarded his tenderness as he wrapped the soft cover around the injured animal, reminding herself that this was a man who normally wore a gun to work and saw some of the toughest sights imaginable in the course of his job. And still he had the gentleness to tend to a wounded puppy.

Quickly he went to his side of the Jeep, climbed in, and started the ignition. The trip to O'Fallon was short, Lee steering carefully around any bump he could avoid to keep from jostling his injured passenger. He let Cassie carry the puppy into the emergency clinic, where a young woman whisked him away to be examined.

"I don't know who owns him, but I'll pick up the bill for now," Lee told the receptionist at the desk.

"Again, Officer Winter? You know you could have just turned him over to Animal Control," she said.

"Yeah, but then you know what would happen to the little fella if nobody claimed him in a week. Keep an eye out for the real owner, and I'll do the same," he said, explaining where they found the pup.

They waited in the lobby until a young vet's assistant came out a few minutes later. "He's got some bumps and bruises, and we're going to X-ray that front leg. I'm guessing it's a single, clean break," the young man said. "Even if it's not broken, we'll need to keep him overnight just to make sure there are no internal injuries. You want to call us in the morning and see if you can take him home?"

"That will be fine," Lee said. "I'll be in touch in the morning."

The assistant complied, and on the way out Lee settled things at the front desk, giving them a number where he could be reached if they needed him. The receptionist acted as if this were a familiar routine.

"Why do I get the feeling this isn't the first rescue for you?" Cassie asked as they walked from the building to the cold parking lot.

"It's pretty obvious, I guess. I can't leave an animal injured on the side of the road. I've always found the owner. Or a new owner. I don't know, though. There's something about this little guy. If nobody claims him, I may take him myself," Lee said, opening the Jeep door for her.

Cassie smiled. "Why do I get the feeling you're already thinking about what to name him?"

Lee's answering grin looked a little sheepish. "Maybe I am. Just maybe." And without another word, he helped her into the Jeep and started the engine.

Five

It was getting easier. Punching in Cassie's number on the phone no longer made Lee feel like he was back in high school, trying to muster the nerve to ask a girl out on a date. He'd gone out with women between those long ago days and now, but there hadn't been a real relationship with one. Not like this. Not where he felt his heart was at stake after a few meetings and one date.

Lee was usually cautious in new situations. Years of police work had seen to that. Normally it was easy to hold back his feelings, staying detached until he had analyzed everything about a person. And by then, he'd have been detached so long it was easy to stay that way.

With Cassie it was another story. He knew he should stay uninvolved with her and the children. Lee tried to tell himself that she was a parent just like the dozens, if not hundreds, of others he ran into in his work with the grade-school kids. Her kids were just like any other set of grade-school siblings who squabbled with each other, were endearing and looked up to him as a role model.

Except telling himself all that wasn't working. He still felt his heart take a funny leap every time he saw her in the halls at Dogwood or called her on the phone. Zach and Sarah brought out a side of him he hadn't felt before, protective and concerned.

It was all happening too fast, Lee told himself. Especially since he couldn't just give his heart to this woman, no matter how lovely and intriguing she was. He had promised himself, long ago, that he wouldn't get involved with anybody who wasn't already a believer. It had been hard enough to get this far on his own journey. Lee wasn't sure if he could go through the sweet pain of surrender with someone else, all over again.

"The best laid plans," he said as he punched up Cassie's number on the phone once more. The little dog, leaning on his knee as they both stretched out on his battered sofa, thumped his tail. "Oh, yeah, Skip," Lee told him, bringing out a small beagle bark just as Cassie answered the phone.

"Well, hello," she said. Her voice was so warm and friendly it made Lee smile. "I don't have to ask who this is. And he's home from the hospital, huh?"

"That he is. And it looks like he's mine, for now at least. I've got four different city departments looking for his former owner."

"How's that going?"

"Nothing so far. I'm beginning to think somebody dumped him," Lee told her. He couldn't imagine why anybody would dump such a beautiful little animal. The dog seemed to sense he was being talked about. He struggled to his feet and walked up to Lee's chest, bestowing wet puppy kisses on his face.

"You should see him. He's got this great neon green cast or splint or whatever on his broken leg. Don't ya, Skippy?"

At the sound of his name, the little dog got even more happily frenzied, yapping so close to the phone that it sent Cassie into laughter. "Skippy? Is that what you named him?"

"He looks like a Skippy. But I've got to stop saying his name. Every time I do, he thinks he's being summoned, and he climbs farther up my chest," Lee told her, pushing the dog gently back down to the sofa so he could breathe and talk.

"All right. So how is you-know-who managing with the cast?"

"Real well. Better than I'm managing. I guess that's why I'm calling, Cassie. This guy needs a family."

There was silence on the line for a moment. "Lee, you know I can't take a dog right now. I'd love to, but…"

"No, not for good," Lee said quickly. "I just need a puppy sitter. I've got some parent meetings next week in the evenings. I can't leave him home alone all day, then at night, too. That's a dangerous thing to do with a, uh, new trainee if you know what I mean."

"That I do. If it's just a puppy sitter you need, we'd be happy to oblige. Any evening you want to drop him off next week would be fine."

Was it Lee's imagination, or did she sound hopeful to see him as well? He decided to find out. "Great. Why don't we start Tuesday? I'll bring Skippy and carry-out pizza for the gang. Would that be okay?"

"Sure. A puppy and pizza. The kids will be thrilled."

"And their mother?" Lee couldn't resist asking.

"Will be delighted not to cook," she added without skipping a beat, which made him smile. "And glad for some adult company during dinner, too."

That sounded promising, Lee decided. He finished the conversation and patted the sleek head of the puppy, who had settled down for another little nap next to him on the couch. "Good dog," he told him.

A dinner date with all the Neels and the puppy sounded like a great idea in theory. But in reality, when Tuesday rolled around, Lee wasn't as sure as he stood on their doorstep balancing pizza boxes in one hand and a wiggling puppy on a leash in the other hand.

The doorbell had hardly finished ringing before the kids opened the door. "Hey, Officer Winter," Zach called. "Come on in."

"Oh, Skippy," Sarah crooned. Her fifth grade cool evaporated as she sat down on the floor near the door to play with the puppy.

"Hi, Lee. Come in and make yourself at home," Cassie called through the fracas. "Let me take those from you."

She relieved him of the pizza boxes as he waded through the pile of children and puppy. Skippy, unsnapped from his leash, was taking turns washing the kids' faces. Lee would have been hard pressed to say who was having the better time.

Cassie motioned him into the kitchen. "This is great. Everybody was so excited about you coming. Zach even cleaned his room in your honor. And I love watching my daughter, Miss Too Cool for Words, making a fool of herself for a dog. It's wonderful to see she is still a little girl when she'll let herself be one."

"It's a funny age," Lee agreed. "And how are you this evening?"

"Grand. I have a weeknight where I don't have to cook, my children were so motivated by having company for dinner that their homework is almost all finished, and I have a dinner companion who won't tell gross jokes at the table or forget to use his napkin."

"My, you do have high standards," Lee teased.

"We try. We really try," Cassie said with a grin. "Now, how about washing up for dinner. Zach, Sarah, you too," she called. "Show Lee where to wash his hands."

Lee dutifully followed the kids down the hall into the bathroom. Cassie watched them all go, hoping that the mayhem would be kept to a minimum with the three of them, and the dog who had followed them, all washing hands in her small hall bath.

She put the pizza on a platter and got out milk and juice while she listened to the jostling and laughing down the hall. Judging from the ruckus, the dog had gotten the end of a roll of toilet tissue while the hand washing happened.

In a moment they were in the kitchen doorway. Cassie was struck by the picture they made. Zach was hanging on Lee's arm, Skippy nipping at one of his socks. Sarah was on Lee's other side, giggling at her brother and the puppy.

They looked so natural. Like a real family, she thought. This was what she'd been missing for so many years, Cassie told herself, fighting back quick tears.

They all got seated at the table, and even as they did, Cassie knew there was more to what she'd been missing than just a family in her kitchen or at her table. She was reminded of what else she had been missing when Lee looked around and reached out his hands to the children on either side of him. "Can we say grace? Is that okay with everybody?"

"Sure," Zach said. "Can I do it?"

Cassie felt her own surprise echoed in Lee's expression. "Go right ahead," she told him, wondering what was coming next. She'd told him and Sarah that Lee would want to give thanks over the food. She'd even found children's books in a stack in the basement that she'd forgotten she had with simple little table graces and beautiful pictures in them. She wasn't sure if either of them had really listened to her story about how she'd learned prayers from those same books, and her grandmother, but apparently Zachary had been listening after all.

Lee took their hands, and Cassie did the same, to complete the circle. "My mom always had us say grace this way. Said it

59

kept the little kids from filching rolls," he said with a grin.

Zach followed Lee's lead in bowing his head, and after a brief pause, he spoke: "Come, Lord Jesus, be our guest. Let these, thy gifts, to us be blessed. Amen."

They all echoed his amen, and Cassie felt a moment of awe. In the early November darkness, lamplight shone on Zach's blond curls. She felt proud of her son and the child's simplicity he showed. Could she be as brave? Could she truly invite Jesus to be a guest at her table, in her life? Perhaps, Cassie thought, with examples like Zach and like Lee, she could find a way to do that. She gave Zach's hand an extra squeeze before letting go and passing the pizza.

Now if he can just get through dinner without sharing any typical third grade table talk, Cassie thought. Perhaps in honor of their very special guest, dinner would be free of the normal interruptions.

It was a charmed meal. No siding salesmen called. The dog curled up and fell asleep on the rug. No drinks were upset, and the conversation would have done Miss Manners proud. Lee even oohed and ahhed appreciatively over the homemade oatmeal cookies Cassie had made for dessert.

"Now this is something I don't get very often," he said. "May I take one for the road, too? I've got to get going in a couple minutes if I'm going to make it to City Hall on time."

"Be my guest," Cassie said. "And leave the table clearing to Zach. It's his turn tonight." Zach sprang up to start his chore much faster than if it had just been the three of them. Cassie smiled, thinking there was more than one reason for having Lee join them for dinner.

"Next time I'll cook," she said, walking him to the front door. "It's hard to believe from what we've done so far, but I really do cook most nights. From scratch, even."

"I can tell," Lee said, waving a cookie. "That's why it's been so much fun to give you a break."

They stood at the doorway, with Cassie wondering how it would feel if he kissed her good-bye. She could imagine it, and her imagination told her it would feel just fine. But not quite yet. She wasn't ready for a kiss, good-bye or otherwise, from Lee. A kiss would say things she wasn't ready to say to anybody. Maybe, for that matter, would never be able to say. Even to Lee.

For now it was enough to stand in the doorway and watch him put on his jacket. "What time will you be back? So we can tell Skippy when he wakes up," she asked, trying to keep her tone light and teasing.

"Around nine-thirty. I hope he doesn't cry or anything. That's what new parents worry about the first time with a baby-sitter, isn't it?" Cassie stifled a laugh. Lee was actually trying to look around the corner into the kitchen where the puppy was sleeping on the rug in front of the sink, oblivious to Zach clearing the table around him.

"It is. And like most new parents, you're going to be late if you stand here worrying. Go," she said, giving him a playful and gentle push. The leather of his jacket was cool to the touch.

"All right. I'll be back soon," he said, finally going.

Ten minutes after he'd left, Skippy woke up. He trotted around the kitchen and living room first, looking for Lee and raising a sweet, questioning face to the rest of them. In the end, it was Sarah he latched on to, sitting in her lap and trying to nibble the ends of her hair while she did homework.

Zach had gone to bed by the time Lee came back, and Cassie and Sarah were settled with their respective piles of paper in the living room. When the knock sounded at the door, Skippy bounded from Sarah's lap.

"Don't open it without looking out," Cassie cautioned.

"Do you think it's anybody else? Look at this dog," Sarah said, pointing to the puppy, wiggling and leaping in front of the door. Still, to please her mother, she looked out first to verify that it was Lee at the door.

"My knees are never going to be the same again," he told Skippy once he bent down to pick up the bounding pup. "You're really glad to see me, aren't you?"

"He was a good boy," Sarah told him. "He didn't even eat my math homework. I tried to get him to, but he doesn't chew paper."

Lee laughed. "Maybe next time. Thanks for keeping an eye on him."

"No problem," Sarah told him. "Anytime you need a dog sitter, Zach and I will be happy to do the job."

"Better ask Mom first," Lee told her. Cassie was thankful that he was the one to say that, and not her. One of the hardest things about being a single parent was always being the heavy. It was such a pleasure to have somebody else fill that role, even for a moment or two.

"Yeah, I guess. But she likes him, too. Don't you, Mom?" Sarah asked, turning to her mother.

"I really do. And he was no trouble," Cassie told Lee, reaching out to stroke Skippy's velvety ears as Lee held him. It was hard to stop there and not admit what her heart was telling her. She was beginning to like Lee Winter, like him quite a bit. And she suspected that liking the owner would get her into far more trouble than liking the squirming brown and white puppy struggling to wash his face.

Six

*I*f only I were two people. That was the only way Cassie could imagine doing everything she needed to do between early November and the first of the year. It was also the only way she could see out of her dilemma regarding Lee Winter.

He seemed to effortlessly weave himself into her life and her children's lives. In a few short weeks, it became impossible to say when Lee had gone from Officer Winter, the guy at school who ran the antidrug education program, to Lee, the guy who helped with homework on the phone, shot baskets, popped for pizza occasionally, and tucked his feet under her kitchen table at least once a week at some time or another.

It seemed almost too simple, too easy. She hadn't had time in her life for a man since Brad died. All her time was spent raising children, earning a living, and doing the thousand small chores around the house and yard. There just wasn't any spare time to date or be involved in a relationship.

Now Lee had slipped into her life and changed all that. He didn't seem to ask for much. A few moments here or there in the hallway at school between classes, a short chat on the phone once the children were in bed for the night. Once in a while, he needed the kids to watch Skippy, who fooled everybody by attaching himself to Cassie instead of to Zach and Sarah.

Sometimes it all seemed too easy. Cassie kept telling herself that this just wouldn't work out in the long run. Lee would want more from her than she could give. In some ways he already did. Not that he asked out loud. It was just something in his attitude, his expectations, that was different.

When she searched her heart, Cassie knew what that something was. Lee was very up-front about being a Christian. His car didn't have any of those bumper stickers she considered obnoxious, and he didn't wear T-shirts with slogans when he was out of uniform. He lived his faith. It shone through his clear eyes. It was in the humble resonance of his voice when he took her hand to say grace. And when Cassie was truthful with herself, she had to admit that Lee's love for God scared her more than anything else when she considered a deepening relationship with Lee Winter.

She didn't know if she could really call herself a Christian anymore. She hadn't been inside a church regularly since Brad's funeral. Even before that, her attendance since her marriage had been spotty. Brad seemed more concerned about "putting in an appearance" in the right clothes, seeing the right people, than he had been with worshipping. His church had never felt like home to Cassie, and once he was gone, she couldn't imagine returning.

She knew the kids were missing out on so many things that she remembered from her childhood, when she went to Sunday school each week with her grandmother. Her own mother had been widowed even younger than Cassie, and she'd taken a variety of jobs to support the two of them, often working weekends. Rather than resenting it, Cassie counted the time as precious because it meant spending more time with Grandma Claire.

But not since then had she really considered herself a faithful Christian. No, Brad had stolen more than just her self-respect, more than just her marriage. He had stolen something far more valuable. Her ability to trust, especially to trust God. Sometimes it haunted her because deep down she knew that God had never deserted her. She just couldn't let him into a heart still filled with anger and hurt.

And when she considered the deepening relationship with Lee, she knew it wasn't fair to saddle him with someone unable to love and believe in God's goodness—acts as natural as breathing to this godly man.

It always came back to this: Any serious relationship with Lee would mean changes in her life, and Cassie wasn't sure she was ready to make those changes.

Still, it was tempting. Lee was fun to be with, and the kids adored him. They would have been thrilled with him even if he hadn't shown up every ten days or so with pizza. But Cassie knew that all that pepperoni didn't hurt either.

At least nobody had taken to feeding the dog under the table. Cassie was thankful for that. She didn't need a fat beagle hanging around. Lee had trained Skippy well. He didn't even beg when he came into the kitchen to watch them eat dinner. Most evenings, he merely curled up on his favorite rug, giving a few deep puppy yawns before falling asleep.

It was a Friday in November, another of Lee's pizza nights, when he made the first invitation for them to come to church with him. There was no big fanfare, just another part of the conversation. Sarah was talking about her student book project and the story she had to write, and Lee mentioned that the Sunday school at his church was having a special event with a storyteller.

"You guys would probably all enjoy it. Why don't I drop by Sunday and we'll go together. I even winterized the Jeep," he said, smiling in Cassie's direction.

The kids chorused their approval, then looked at Cassie with questions in their eyes. If she said no now, she would feel like an ogre.

"Sure. But I don't know if we've really got the right kind of clothes for church, especially Zach," she began before Lee waved away her objections.

"Not a problem. We aren't ever terribly dressy. And tomorrow will be especially casual with everybody getting together to hear the storyteller," he said. "Is it all right? I guess I should have asked you alone before I mentioned it in front of these two, but I just thought of it...."

"It's fine, really," Cassie said, feeling tension tighten her shoulders. "Just let me know what time to be ready."

When Sunday morning came, Cassie was ready on the outside. The inside was another matter. Her morning had been spent making sure the children were clean and in good clothes that all matched, and that she looked presentable herself. They had a quick cold cereal breakfast and were waiting when Lee came to whisk them away.

Driving up to the big brick structure, Cassie felt panicky. What if Zach said something awful? What if Sarah pulled one of her preteen conniption fits and sat and rolled her eyes and acted as if it was all the silliest thing she'd seen in weeks? What if she herself had forgotten how to act in church?

Lee seemed to sense her discomfort. "We'll all be fine," he said softly as he pulled into a parking space. "You just wait and see."

He came around and opened Cassie's door, and they all walked up to the church. "In this way, then down those stairs to Fellowship Hall," he directed the kids. "Your mom and I will be right behind you. If we stop, it will be to get a cup of coffee."

"Okay. I think I saw Jenny from school," Sarah said, motioning her brother down the stairs. "Come on with me, and let's see."

"That was painless enough, wasn't it?" Lee asked, helping Cassie down the stairs. "Your hands are cold."

"I'm nervous. It's been so long since I've been in a church," Cassie admitted.

"Most of us are pretty friendly folks," Lee told her with a grin, then headed for the coffee urn. He poured them each a cup of coffee and handed one to Cassie. "This should bolster you a little bit. Let's find some seats before the storyteller starts."

He craned his neck, looking for the right place. "The kids are up front," he told Cassie. "We could sit with them, but it appears Sarah did find a friend from school. And Zach is talking to somebody like he knows him."

"That's a possibility. Zach always finds somebody he knows wherever we go," Cassie said. "We can sit back with the other grown-ups as long as the kids know where we are."

"Fine. I'll go tell them, and you can keep me a place," Lee said, pointing to two folding chairs on the end of a row. Cassie settled into her seat and waited for Lee to come back.

While she waited, she looked around the room. It was a large hall, almost an auditorium. Bright and cheerful, the walls were covered with posters and children's drawings. In the front of the room was a table with what appeared to be stacks of clothing and some ordinary household items, and several chairs had been arranged next to a microphone. All around her people sat, talking to their neighbors, drinking coffee. Several smiled at her and called out friendly greetings.

They looked just like the crowd at a PTA meeting or one of Zach's soccer practices, except dressed a little better. Cassie began to feel that maybe she wasn't so out of place after all.

Lee slid in next to her. "The troops are alerted. I think I got 'the look' from Sarah for letting her know where we are."

"Did she roll her eyes as if no one could possibly mistake her for someone infantile enough to need to know the whereabouts of her mother?" Cassie asked, trying not to laugh.

Lee nodded. "That's it."

Cassie patted him on the shoulder. "Congratulations. I do believe this makes you an honorary parent or something. Not everyone gets 'the look.'"

"I'm honored. I think," Lee said, his expression wry.

Before they could say anything more, the Sunday school superintendent stepped up to the microphone, introduced himself, and introduced the storyteller. She was a small woman in her fifties, and Cassie worried at first that her voice would be too soft to hear even with the microphone.

Then she started talking, and Cassie needn't have worried. Her words bubbled forth with such enthusiasm that even the little children sitting on carpet squares in the front of the room quieted down and stopped wiggling.

The props on the table went through the lady's hands, one by one. They were such normal, ordinary things, but she made them into something magical. A plaid bathrobe became the robe of Joseph, wrapped around a giggling six-year-old from the front row who marched around while the storyteller kept his contemporaries spellbound with her retelling of Joseph's trip to Egypt, and his rise to Pharaoh's right-hand man.

Several other props took their turn, leaving just one, a big bag of dog food. Cassie's eyes kept straying to it, wondering what the lady would do with it. Finally she found out.

"Well, I've still got one thing left," the storyteller said, motioning toward the bag. "Anybody hungry? Want a little snack?"

"Eeew. Gross!" the little children in the front row called out.

"Well, you never know," the storyteller told them. "If you got hungry enough, it might taste good."

"I've never been that hungry," one little girl piped up.

"Good," the storyteller told her. "But I know of someone who was. He was a rich young man. One day he went to his father and told him that he didn't want to wait around for years and years for his father to die before he got his inheritance."

It was the story of the prodigal son. Cassie sat on the edge of her chair, listening attentively. It was almost as if she'd never heard the story before, because somehow the woman was telling it to *her.* There was so much in her life that was like that rich young man who walked away from home and spent his inheritance on high living.

When she'd married Brad, he'd become the center of her life. She, too, had "squandered" that inheritance from her early years of trusting God, believing in his mercy, his love.

And then there was that young man, tending pigs after his money ran out, and so hungry that the pig slop looked good. The storyteller had that bag of dog food open by now and cascaded a handful through her fingers, bringing another chorus of "Eeew" and "Yuck" from the carpet-square brigade. Cassie could feel the young man's anguish in the storyteller's words.

"'I'll go home,' the young man said. 'But my dad won't want me back for a son. I could be a servant, I guess. Even my dad's servants get fed better than these pigs. That's what I'll do. I'll go home.'"

Cassie could feel tears rising to the surface. She had been away from home so long herself. Away from church, away from God, away from anything that reminded her of him.

Now here was this quiet, unassuming lady telling a story that seemed to be her own. And here, sitting beside her, was Lee. When had she taken his hand? It was warm and comforting, such a reassurance to know that he was there. It seemed to be a little message from God. *I'm here,* that hand squeeze seemed to say. *I've always been here. Why don't you come home too, Cassie?*

She listened to the storyteller. Marvelously, at the end of the story, there was the Father, with a hug and a ring and the best robe.

Cassie didn't realize she was crying until Lee put an arm around her and handed her a tissue. "I didn't want it to get to you this way, really," he said softly.

"I know. But it did. And I'm so glad, Lee, really," she told him. "There's just so much…" Her voice faltered.

Instead of answering, he nodded in understanding and kissed her cheek softly. Cassie had to wipe away another tear or two. Like the prodigal, she was taking her first steps home. Not just to a building like this church, but to her Father. And it felt so very good.

Later, when the crowd around the storyteller had thinned, Cassie walked to the front and introduced herself. "I haven't been to church in a long, long time. I was afraid I was going to feel strange and unwelcome. But listening to you made me long for something I've been missing in my life," she said, her eyes misting. "Maybe I should say, Someone."

The storyteller reached out and hugged the younger woman. "I'm so happy to hear that. Sometimes it seems like I'm just telling the same old stories to people who have heard them a thousand times. This morning—as I do many times—before I started to speak, I prayed for that one person I knew that God would touch." She smiled into Cassie's eyes. "You're that person, Cassie."

Cassie choked on her tears and nodded. The storyteller gave her another hug. "God bless you, dear," she whispered, "as you begin your journey home."

Lee stood to one side, waiting for her. "You up for services upstairs?" he asked gently as she walked toward him.

Cassie smiled, feeling a warmth and joy she hadn't experienced in a long time. "Today I feel up for anything. Let's gather the kids and go. You sit next to Zach to show him the ropes. He'll need the most help."

Lee gave her a look that reminded her of the puppy. "But I wanted to sit next to you."

"You have two sides, silly," she said, her heart lighter than she knew was possible. "I'll sit on one, and Zach can sit on the other. That way we can put Sarah on the other side of me, putting the most distance possible between the kids."

Lee laughed. "You haven't forgotten everything about going to church."

"Not everything," she agreed. "I had boy cousins Zach's age. And a very wise grandmother."

A few minutes later, Cassie stepped through the doors into the sanctuary. Although this was another place, another time from Grandma Claire's church so long ago, it felt like home.

She could hardly wait to see what this homecoming would be like.

Seven

Cassie felt as if she were floating on air for several days after going to church with Lee. It was such a different experience. The kids had a lot of questions, but they wanted to go back. She began to regret all the years she'd missed taking them to church. When Sarah found out about the youth group activities that Lee's church offered for middle schoolers and above, she had another reason to look forward to turning twelve. And Zach, who never met a stranger anyway, was excited about all the new people he'd have to play with if he went to Sunday school.

It was all moving so fast, though. Being with Lee and fitting into his life made Cassie a little nervous. She didn't realize just how nervous until Dierdre called one evening.

It was only after she'd been on the phone for a few minutes that Cassie realized she hadn't talked to Dierdre since she'd started seeing Lee. She would have to have a little chat with the children to talk to them about how Grandma would perceive her having a "boyfriend" before they talked to her. No matter how it was presented, Cassie knew what Dierdre's reaction would be. She'd go through the roof. Her perfect son couldn't be replaced.

Still, Cassie tried to remain calm and make small talk while Dierdre talked about the children. "Will I be seeing them over Thanksgiving?" she asked. She asked every year, and every year the answer was the same. Cassie bit her tongue for a moment to keep from snapping and tried to sound sweet.

"They only have the four days off from school. If you'd like to come here and have Thanksgiving with us, you'd certainly be welcome, " Cassie said.

"No, I know there's no guest room in that little house, and I hate to put anybody out. Besides, the weather is so iffy this time of year," Dierdre said with a sniff. "I do miss the holidays with my family, though."

"I know you do. How about taking the train?" Cassie asked.

"Traveling alone just isn't comfortable for me," Dierdre replied. "I'll just wait until Christmas when we can meet in Columbia and I can have my angels for a few days. I can always roast a chicken for Thanksgiving. With just me and perhaps Mrs. Phillips from church, it wouldn't make any sense to have a turkey. I'd be eating leftovers forever."

"We really would love to have you," Cassie said, one more time. Perhaps having Dierdre there, in person, would be the way to introduce her to Lee.

"No, really, I couldn't," Dierdre answered. Then she paused a moment. "Cassie, is that a dog I hear? Surely you haven't gotten the children a dog?"

Having Skippy was so much a part of the evening routine that Cassie had forgotten he was in the kitchen playing ball with Zach. "It is a dog. But it isn't ours," Cassie told her. "We're dog sitting for a friend, just for the evening."

"Good. For a moment I was afraid you'd actually gotten an animal. And you know how allergic Bradley was to anything with fur. Surely the children inherited that."

Like they inherited anything worth talking about from him, Cassie said silently to herself. "They haven't shown any signs of allergy yet, but Skippy is just visiting," she said out loud.

"Well, that's good. You're keeping him in the kitchen, I hope. No sense getting fleas in the carpets."

Fleas! As if Lee's dog would have fleas. "This particular little guy is well taken care of. He does stay in the kitchen most of the time when he's here, just because he's still a puppy," Cassie said. "But I'm sure you didn't call to talk about a dog."

"Certainly not. When does the children's Christmas break start?"

"The twenty-third of December," Cassie said. "I expected we'd be meeting in Columbia the twenty-sixth, as usual."

"Weather permitting," Dierdre said. "You know I don't drive in snow or ice. But otherwise, nothing could keep me from my time with my darlings. I suppose you'll want them back for New Year's?"

"I think so. It's a little rough on them to travel one day and have to go to school the next," Cassie said. She could have had this conversation in her sleep. It hadn't varied in years.

"I suppose. It would be so nice if I could keep them...keep them a little longer, I mean," she paused for just a heartbeat. "Be thinking of things they would like for Christmas. I've gotten some of their big presents, but there's always those little stocking stuffers."

Why didn't Dierdre just annoy her twice, Cassie thought? Point out the fabulous amount of money she had to spend on the children at Christmas, and point out that her shopping was already done a week before Thanksgiving both at the same time. Ah, well, if there was any way she could make Cassie feel inadequate twice, she'd find a way. "I'll keep it in mind, Dierdre," Cassie said.

"None of those awful video games for Zach. And you're certainly not letting little Sarah wear makeup and pantyhose yet, I hope?"

Cassie stifled a sigh. "Just perfume. And colored tights. She is still a little girl most of the time."

"Good. I'm sure that public school environment doesn't help. I see them all the time, you know, children her age roaming in packs at the mall, tiny little skirts and enough mascara to look like raccoons...."

"Well, you'd never see Sarah that way," Cassie said, hearing the fear in the older woman's voice for the first time. With a twinge of guilt, she wondered if the rediscovery of her Father's love might be causing her to see Dierdre in a new light. She narrowed her eyes in thought, listening to the concern in the older woman's voice.

Zach and Sarah were Dierdre's only real family. She might not approve of how they were being raised, or schooled, and no matter how she rankled Cassie, she cared about the children. Cared a lot.

"She just isn't that kind of girl, nor would I let her be," Cassie said, her voice softer.

"I'm sure you wouldn't," Dierdre went on. She didn't sound all that convinced to Cassie, but for once she decided to take her statement at face value. "I'll let you go. You probably have several loads of laundry to do, and more housekeeping since you don't get to do it during the daytime. And then there's all that dog hair in your kitchen." She said her good-byes and left Cassie laughing for once instead of fuming.

Putting down the phone and going to the kitchen, Cassie first whispered a prayer of thanksgiving to God for softening her heart toward Dierdre. Then she resolved to begin that talk with Zach, the one about "What to say to Grandma about

76

Officer Winter." This was going to be almost as interesting as the conversation she'd just had with Dierdre.

"You remembered, didn't you?" Zach asked a few nights later at the dinner table. Outside, a thunderstorm that had rumbled in after school poured steady sheets of rain. It was the kind of night to stay inside, snug and dry.

"Remembered what?" Cassie asked, as another clap of thunder rolled in the distance. "I've got your favorite sweatshirt in the dryer, and I know you want to bring your lunch tomorrow."

"No, the Thanksgiving feast," he said, with a mothers-are-hopeless sigh. "You remembered the Thanksgiving feast tomorrow for my class, didn't you?"

"Is that tomorrow already? What are you supposed to bring?" Cassie asked.

"Just paper plates and napkins, Mom. I didn't sign you up for anything hard."

"Good, Zachary, because you also didn't write it on the calendar, and you know what that means."

"It doesn't get done," chorused both children. The Dogwood school calendar posted on the kitchen bulletin board was Cassie's command center. It noted everything that everybody was supposed to bring to school, odd times to be places, the works. And now she had a little problem.

"I'm going to have to go out after supper and get those things for you, Zach, I'm out of both," she told him. The rain pounded down outside, and Cassie sighed, thinking about leaving the house for a mad dash to the store.

"It doesn't have to be fancy ones with turkeys on them or anything, Mom," Zach said, eager not to cause trouble.

"I know, Zachary, but look around. I don't even have anything nonfancy tonight."

"Yeah, I had to use paper towels to set the table for dinner. Good thing Lee wasn't coming tonight, huh, Mom?" Sarah pointed out.

"Good thing," Cassie agreed. "I hope it stops raining so I don't have to drive in this mess." But the rain didn't stop. It didn't even slack off. An hour after dinner, the thunder still rumbled, and lightning still flickered through the curtained windows.

Finally Cassie grabbed the car keys and gave Sarah instructions on watching her brother. She couldn't delay the trip any longer or she'd be running into bedtime, and that wasn't something she wanted to do.

She dashed to the nearest grocery store, got the paper plates and napkins, and a gallon of milk just to be on the safe side. The rain hadn't slowed down any as she splashed across the parking lot to her car. In fact, there were deep puddles beginning to form on the parking lot where the drains couldn't handle the water. "Great," Cassie muttered. She hated driving in heavy rainstorms, even the few blocks to her home.

Still, she started the car and headed out, determined to get home before bedtime for the children. When she got to the one major intersection between the store and home, there was a lineup waiting. All the traffic signals were flashing, and several cars waited to go through the almost-flooded roadway. Cassie sighed, waiting her turn. To the side, a police officer in rain gear waved the traffic through.

"Come on," she muttered to the line of traffic. "I want to get home." Finally it was her turn, and she moved the car slowly through the standing water.

She was halfway through the intersection before she realized that something was very wrong. Her car was moving through the intersection just fine, but so was the pickup truck coming right at her. And he wasn't going to stop!

"Lord, help me!" Cassie cried as the truck plowed into her car.

The horrible sound of rending glass and metal seemed to last forever. When the awful noise stopped, and Cassie shakily looked around, all she could see in the darkness was glass and bent metal folding in on the passenger side of her little car. Outside the rain continued to fall, and she shuddered again.

The police officer was at her side immediately, helping her from the car. "Is there anyone I can call for you?" he asked when things settled down on the scene. He'd already taken her statement and that of the truck driver, whose brakes had apparently failed in the rain.

"No, not really. My kids are home alone," Cassie began, before a picture of Lee's face flashed in her mind. "Wait a minute. Yes, there is," Cassie said. She wasn't hurt badly, and there was no need to go to the hospital. But the car was a wreck. Looking at the mashed-in passenger side, she suspected it was totalled.

She made two phone calls, one to Lee, who was home and promised to come right away, and one to Sarah, just to tell her that she was going to be late coming home. She didn't let her know the extent of the accident, making it sound more like an inconvenience than a calamity. There would be time to tell her the whole truth when Cassie came home and was obviously unhurt.

There was glass in her hair from the shattered windshield. And she could tell she would be sore tomorrow from being bounced around a little inside the car. Thank goodness she was wearing a seat belt.

Lee was there quickly. He seemed to have been relaxing at home because this was the first time she'd seen him in blue jeans and a sweatshirt. Even slightly rumpled in his casual clothes, he looked wonderful. From the moment he got on the scene, Cassie relaxed a little. Lee would know what to do. He made sure the insurance information from the driver of the truck was in order, and that Cassie really didn't want to go to the hospital. He made it clear what he thought of that choice but didn't press the issue. He made sure the tow truck driver had been called to take the car to a nearby auto repair shop where it could be assessed for damages for the insurance companies. And like Cassie, he didn't hold out much hope that it was salvageable.

When all that remained of the accident was a pile of broken glass in the street, he put an arm around her shoulder. "Now can I take you home?" he asked.

"With pleasure," she told him. Sarah was a little disturbed when they arrived home without her mom's car. However, Lee helped reassure her that nothing was terribly wrong.

"This weekend we'll go out shopping for new wheels for your mom," he told the girl, ruffling her hair. "And until then, you can rely on Uncle Lee's taxi service whenever I'm available."

"Okay," Sarah said doubtfully. "Does this mean I have to go to bed, now that you're home?"

"It does," Cassie told her. "I'll come tuck you in." For the most part, Sarah had outgrown being tucked in, preferring to read in bed for a little while before lights out. But tonight Cassie felt they both needed the slower pace. So she went into Sarah's room, which was slowly making the transition from Barbie pink to teenager eclectic, and settled her under the puffy comforter.

"Were you scared, Mom?" she asked, her eyes bright as she looked up at Cassie.

It was with surprise that Cassie found her answer. "You know, I wasn't. There wasn't much time to be scared. And you know what else surprised me? Just before that truck hit the car, I said a prayer." It surprised her that it had been uttered in a way as natural to her as breathing. And in that awful moment of impact, Cassie had not felt alone in the little car.

She kissed Sarah good night and walked in to where Lee was settling Zach down next door. He was giving him all the gritty male details of the wreck without dramatizing any, telling him about the size of the tow truck and the litter of broken glass in the street. "Which we still have to get out of your mom's hair before she goes to sleep, so you better call it a night, Zach," Lee said, patting his shoulder. "I'll leave Mom to do the mushy stuff."

Cassie did the "mushy stuff," feeling very grateful that she was here and whole to kiss her children good night and came out of the bedroom. "How do we do that? Get the broken glass out of my hair? I can feel it in there, you know. It feels like a million little gritty things in there."

"Have you got a pair of pantyhose you're done with?" Lee asked.

"Sure. The ones I'm wearing. They're in shreds. I didn't notice it until we were waiting for the tow truck," Cassie said.

"Go take them off and bring them back here with a pair of scissors and the part of your shower drain that's removable, if it is," Lee told her.

It sounded strange to Cassie, but she did just that. Lee cut a leg off the pantyhose and wrapped it around the drain cover. "Now, fit this back on, letting that loose tail trail free on the shower floor. And wear beach shoes in that shower for the next couple times you wash your hair."

"We've got one more job to do before I let you in there. I need a sheet and a comb," he told her. Spreading the sheet out on the floor, he had Cassie sit in a kitchen chair and lean her head over the sheet. Then he combed her hair from the roots

81

out. She could hear pieces of glass plop onto the sheet in a miniature rainstorm.

It was looking at the pile of glass on the sheet, once he was done combing, that finally unnerved her. The tears came out of nowhere, and Lee gathered her into his arms, murmuring soft words while she stood in the middle of her kitchen floor and cried.

It was there that she said her second prayer of the night, this one silent but just as fervent. *Thank you for this good man,* she told God, as the "good man" wrapped his arms around her and soothed her. He was so solid and warm. His sweatshirt smelled slightly of wood smoke and aftershave as she buried her face in it, and his strong hands cradled her there. There was a huskiness to his voice, almost a catch in it as he soothed her the way he might an edgy toddler. "It's going to be okay," Lee told her. And in his embrace, Cassie could believe it.

Eight

olding Cassie in his arms, Lee felt torn. For her sake, he wanted her to calm down and stop crying so that she'd feel better. For his own, he wanted to hold her in his arms forever. It felt so good, so right, for her to nestle in his arms. He hated to release her for any reason.

"You needed to do that, you know," he told her once her breathing had slowed to near normal and the tears had stopped.

"I know, I probably did," Cassie said, using the back of her hand to wipe away tears. "But I hate doing it, especially in front of anybody."

Lee felt a pang of hurt. "So I'm just anybody now, huh?"

Cassie gave him a shaky laugh. "No, you're much more than that, Lee. But you know what I mean."

Lee looked down at her, still enclosed in the circle of his arms. "I do know. Now ask me if I approve."

Cassie pulled away, a guarded look crossing her face. "What are you getting at?"

"Always taking care of yourself. Trying to be Supermom. It

doesn't have to be that way, you know," he said, trying to be as gentle as possible.

Cassie's face became even more closed. "I don't need anybody else to take care of me. The one time I made that mistake, it turned out badly."

"With Brad, you mean?" All Lee knew about Brad was what Cassie had told him and what he remembered from that night six years before. It wasn't much.

"With Brad," she said.

"Well, I'm not Brad. And I didn't mean just me anyway, Cassie." He reached out and touched her cheek. It was so incredibly soft, like a child's. "I was talking about letting God take some of that burden. It has to get awful heavy when you're carrying it alone."

Cassie turned away, frowning. "God isn't going to file insurance claims for me, or get me to work while my car's in the shop. So I better be self-reliant just a little longer, hadn't I?"

Lee felt her hurt. "No, he won't do all that, Cass. But he'll be there while you do it. There's no situation so bad that the Father leaves us alone to face it, if we just ask for help. I know that isn't easy. Sometimes it's the hardest thing in the world."

"Is it? Have you ever been there?" Cassie snapped. "You, with your perfect faith. Nothing ever scares you, does it, Lee?"

He looked at her in surprise. "Are you kidding? I'm probably terrified on the average of once a week, and at least mildly scared once a day. And don't make the mistake of thinking I'm perfect, Cassie. I'm not all that much farther along in all this searching than you are, and it took a calamity to get me started on the path."

"You?" Her brow wrinkled. "It always seems that everything comes so naturally for you."

"I was raised a believer, and I never really fell away from the church," Lee said. "But everything about God and my religion was just something I took for granted. Church was someplace I went with my family when I came home for a holiday. And then I got shot."

"Shot?" Cassie's eyes filled with concern. "You never said anything before about being shot."

"It was not too long after I left the patrol. I was working Narcotics and was part of a drug buy gone bad. One moment I was facing a man with a gun. The next thing I remember was coming out of surgery. It was a clean hit, high in the shoulder. No major organ damage or anything."

"But you were shot."

"Definitely. And I had a few days to lie in a hospital bed and think about my life. I didn't like it the way it was. But my thoughts kept returning to the shooting itself. I could remember a quick, whispered prayer before I passed out. It sounds strange, but I knew in that instant there was Someone with me. A Presence that told me no matter what happened, everything would be all right. I decided that once I got out of the hospital, I really wanted to know who that Someone really was."

"And do you know?" The upward tilt to Cassie's chin looked stubborn.

"I know a lot more than I did before I got shot," Lee said. "Do I know everything? Understand everything? I never will, not in this lifetime. There is so much we have to leave in God's hands, Cass. If anything, I guess I can say that now I'm more content to leave it there."

"Okay," Cassie said. "I can appreciate that. But I have to admit that I'm pretty comfortable relying on my own two hands, Lee. I guess I'm just not quite ready for what you're suggesting."

Lee felt hurt but not surprised. He knew how difficult it was to let God take control. "Okay," he said gently after a moment. "Maybe it's time I went home so you can rest. Please take something for muscle soreness before you go to bed."

"It's going to be that bad?"

"You tense up in all kinds of places during an accident and after. You'll be lucky to get out of bed in the morning," he told her.

They walked to the door. "I'm sorry I snapped at you," Cassie said as they stood on the threshold.

Lee waved off her apology. "No problem. I'll pray for you, Cass. And I'll be back in the morning to help out if you need me," he told her. "Good night."

It seemed so quiet once Lee was gone. The children were asleep and it was late. Cassie called the hotline number at school. At first she was just going to tell the machine that she'd be in late. But while listening to the recording, she decided that Lee was probably right. She told Sandy's soothing recording that she was going to take the day off to handle all the aggravation of the accident and to go to the doctor's office if necessary. Message completed, she hung up and headed off to bed.

In the morning she was very glad that she'd already taken the day off. Rolling out of bed felt as if she'd been hit by a pile of bricks. Gingerly, she dressed in old sweats and did what she needed to get the children off to school, sending them with a neighbor who didn't mind driving. Then, with a mug of tea in her hand, she settled down on the couch to feel like a flu victim for a little while and assess all the phone calls she was going to have to make.

By the time she was done with her calling, about an hour later, she felt as if the phone ought to be grafted to her ear. The news wasn't great from anybody. Fortunately, her insurance coverage was good, and she'd never had so much as a dent before. The driver of the truck was insured as well, and given the nature of the police report, his company would probably be bearing the brunt of the damages.

But the auto repair shop was as pessimistic as she feared they would be. Her beloved little hatchback was totaled. And because it wasn't new or large, she would have to shop hard to replace it on what the insurance companies would give her.

"It's car loan time for sure," she said with a sigh, seeing her dream of going back to school slip farther from reach. Again. Of course she could always call Dierdre and tell her what was happening. Cassie sighed again. She'd rather sell body parts than admit to Dierdre that she was having money problems.

Before lunch she found herself stretched out on the couch, taking a nap. She really felt as if she'd had a bad case of the flu; nothing else had ever left her this sore and drained.

The phone ringing woke her up some time later. Cassie struggled out of her afghan and answered. It was Lee. She could tell from the background noise that he was probably calling from the teachers' lounge at school.

"How's my best girl?" he asked, causing a feeling of warmth to wash over Cassie at his words. "I'm glad you decided to stay home. I would have suggested it myself, but—"

"But you were probably afraid of having me come any closer to biting your head off than I already did," Cassie said. "I wasn't the best of company last night, I know."

"Didn't expect you to be," Lee said. "Nobody who's been in a car accident has to be good company for at least twenty-four hours. It's the rules. Didn't you know?"

"No, but I won't argue," Cassie said, pushing her hair away from her face. She told him about the situation with her car. "Guess I'll be hoofing it for a few days. It's kind of nice that it will be a holiday and we won't have to worry about much."

"That's one of the reasons I was calling," Lee said. "I found out that one of the guys on days is selling a nice little sedan cheap. He just made detective and he gets an unmarked. He's got a car at home he's not going to need. I told him not to offer it to anybody else until we could take a look at it."

Cassie felt so touched that tears sprang to her eyes. "That's so sweet. Thanks."

"Hey, anytime, I figure I'm doing you both a favor. It should be a nice car for you, and George wouldn't have to go through the hassle of selling it himself this way. How about I pick you up about four to go see it. And by the way, this is definitely a pizza night."

"I won't argue," Cassie said. "You are terribly good to me." It was only after she hung up that Cassie realized that when Lee had called her his "best girl," he'd been in the crowded faculty lounge on a public phone. She might have to do something about that. And then again, she thought, smiling before she drifted off to sleep again, she just might not.

By the time the kids were ferried home from school, Cassie felt more like her regular self. She had gotten up, showered again (still finding a few little remnants of that broken glass, which Lee had warned her about), and put on jeans and a sweater.

She'd made a few more phone calls, chiefly to the teachers' credit union where she was a member, to see if she could get a temporary loan if George's little car turned out to be something she wanted. Even on her small income they seemed happy to help her out, given the circumstances. When it started to rain again shortly before the kids got home, she was thankful that her neighbor had offered to bring them home as well as take them to school. They dashed into the house, holding book bags over their heads instead of the umbrellas they never packed.

For a change Cassie got to see what the other moms went through in that hectic fifteen minutes after school let out. It was unusual to have the two of them telling her all about their days.

Usually she'd been there for most of them, or at least seen some of the events unfold. Sitting at the kitchen table with cookies, hearing all about everything was a different experience. Cassie decided that given a choice, she liked her usual way better.

So, it appeared, did most of the teachers whose classrooms she visited. Sarah's book bag was full of "hurry back soon" notes from different classrooms. Cassie never thought about anybody missing her before. She never considered what she did as such a valuable service. To read the notes from the teachers, she had to think otherwise. All in all, staying home for one day was an eye-opening experience. Not one she was anxious to repeat, especially given the circumstances, but enlightening just the same.

Lee called about four, as everyone was polishing off the cookie crumbs. "Want to go look at a car? George should be home about five, and he said to come on over if we want."

"Sure," Cassie said. "If you want to come over before that, you're welcome. I'm much better company than I was last night."

"Great. I'll see you in a few minutes," Lee said. True to his word, it was about fifteen minutes later when there was a knock at the door.

Cassie was still touched by the way Lee came into her house. He didn't just walk in and sit down, instead finding each and every member of the family that he knew to be home and saying hello, asking about their day. Only afterward did he accept Cassie's offer to sit down at the kitchen table and have a few of the remaining cookies and a glass of milk. "I haven't had an after-school snack in a while," he said with a grin. "Thanks."

"It's not usually a big deal here either, but it was so different today being here when the kids came home from school, instead of bringing them home myself, that I decided to do things differently," she said.

Cassie caught him up on everything she'd done that day, and Lee told her a little about how his day's DARE classes had gone. It felt so comfortable to be sitting here with him. This was one of the parts of having Lee around that she liked best; having another adult to talk to once in a while.

"I love watching you work around the kitchen," he told her after she'd gotten up and put their few dishes in the dishwasher and wiped down all the surfaces.

"I'm really better in the classroom," Cassie admitted.

"I know, but I don't get to see you there. And you just have such a style to your movements," he said, smiling ruefully. "That sounds a little awkward, not really the way I wanted it to." Then he added with a slight grimace, "I guess I'm not used to giving a woman compliments."

"It sounded pretty good to me. Of course, I'm not used to receiving them, except the kind that come from grade-school-age children, so we'll get along fine in that respect," Cassie said. She had the most tremendous urge to walk over to where he sat in her kitchen and kiss him.

Instead, she looked at the clock on the microwave. "Five o'clock. Should we go see your friend George?"

"We should," Lee said. "Let's round up the kids and get going."

The kids were a little excited to go look at a car. They were less excited when Cassie told them they weren't going to a dealership with a big screen TV to watch but would be expected to sit in Lee's car most of the time while the adults looked over another vehicle. Still, they weren't too put out and didn't even squabble and punch each other in the quest for possession of the back seat, for which Cassie was thankful.

In the end, George's sedan was perfect. It might not be Cassie's dream car, like the shiny minivans a lot of her coworkers with children drove, but it was serviceable, dent free, and had low mileage. The kids fit well in the back seat, and George, who looked like a family man himself, seemed to get a kick out of watching them bounce in and out of it.

"That's the reason we got a four door at the time," he said, running his hand over the fender, slightly damp from the recent rain. "Now we've got teenagers and it doesn't matter because they never want to ride with the old folks anyway."

Lee was under the hood of the car, looking at things that Cassie could only identify on the surface. She joined him for a minute. "I really like this car. Do you think he'll let me take it for a spin?"

"That's the idea," Lee told her, getting the keys from his friend. They went around a couple blocks, with Cassie taking it out on one of the main roads so that she could test it out at higher speeds as well. In fifteen minutes she was fairly sure that if George would sell her the car, she would be happy to buy it.

"Now we have to talk price," she told him inside, in a family room complete with a golden retriever, who was keeping the kids occupied by going to first one and then the other and putting a large front paw in their laps, asking to be petted.

He named a figure that seemed low to Cassie. "Are you sure?" she asked.

"It's all I need from it. And for a friend of Lee's, I can't see asking more. He's gotten me out of a few scrapes over the years. Don't want him thinking twice next time," George joked.

"It will probably be Monday before I can pick it up," Cassie told him. "It will take the credit union that long to get my loan set up, and let me go in and sign all the papers."

George held up a hand. "Leave me a deposit and take it home for the weekend. I don't want you stranded with those kids over Thanksgiving."

Cassie was amazed. "Are you sure?"

"Positive. I know where you live. And I definitely know

where this guy lives. That's good enough for me."

Half an hour later, she was driving home in her new car, still feeling a little dazed. In little more than an hour's time, she had bought a new car and settled all the payment and was driving it home. None of it would have been possible without Lee. *None of it would have been possible without God, either,* a little voice in her head told her. But she pushed that one away for the time being. That was a little too heavy for her to handle at the moment. But driving into the garage in her new car, she knew in her heart that it was true.

Nine

"What are you doing for Thanksgiving?" Cassie asked Lee as he toyed with the last of the pizza crusts on his plate that night.

"Coming here?" He had a very hopeful look on his face. "If you're even fixing anything. I know this has been a pretty stressful week."

"There's a turkey thawing in the refrigerator even as we speak. Nothing will be terribly fancy, but it will have all the elements of a traditional Thanksgiving dinner," Cassie said, smiling. She hesitated just a moment before continuing. "I figured you'd have a dozen invitations."

"I do. And I've been politely declining all of them, including one to George's tomorrow, in hopes that you'd ask me here."

"Why didn't you say something sooner?" Cassie asked. "For all I knew, you could have been going home, wherever home is."

"A little too far to go just for Thanksgiving," Lee said. "At least anymore. My folks used to live not too far from here, but my youngest sister settled in Mobile, and Dad especially liked the year round golfing and fishing there. So they moved down that way a few years ago. I do go see them, and they still come up here for visits. But not for Thanksgiving."

"I'm planning on dinner about four. Will that fit into your plans?"

Lee smiled. "Since I'm pretty much plan-free, it will fit fine."

"Good. Bring Skippy," Cassie told him. "He's one of those blessings I'm thankful for this year."

"I will. Maybe I can even talk him into wearing a bow."

"Good luck," Cassie said, picturing a bow after ten minutes on the wiggly puppy. Somehow this sounded like a recipe for a miniature disaster. But Lee was welcome to try. If anybody she knew could get Skippy to sit still for dressing up, it was the handsome man at her kitchen table. She was beginning to think he could do just about anything he put his mind to.

That night after Lee went home, Cassie started getting ready for Thanksgiving dinner. She peeled potatoes to put in water in the refrigerator, cut up raw vegetables for a relish tray, and made sure the turkey was really thawing so that she could put it in the oven the next day. As she worked she thought, long and hard.

She had to admit it. She was falling in love with Lee Winter. He was everything she could have asked for in a man...if she had been asking, or even looking. As it was, he'd come out of the blue. Cassie wasn't looking for a man in her life, but there was Lee. She couldn't imagine that anyone as wonderful as Lee could be interested in her.

And he was single. Truly single, never having been married. Probably his expectations from a wife would be different than what she'd experienced with Brad. She couldn't go back to the person she'd been, married to Bradley. She wasn't ready to do that, now or ever. Even though the last six years had been hard, filled with struggle and lack of money, they'd taught her so much. She knew what she could do now and how much she enjoyed doing it for herself. And she wasn't ready to go back to being less than that just to please a man.

Cassie put the container of raw vegetables in the refrigerator and mentally shook herself. Who said Lee Winter was looking for somebody to be the perfect little stay-at-home wife? He seemed genuinely interested in her plans to be a teacher. He was more hopeful than Cassie that she'd actually achieve her goal.

Cassie got out frozen bread dough, prepared a pan, and put a loaf to rise for the morning. She knew what the biggest problem to falling in love with Lee Winter would be. Lee lived his faith and trusted God for every decision he made, every breath he took.

And Cassie didn't know if she was ready to let God take control of her life. It was one thing to see God as her loving Father, accepting her back "home," just as he had the prodigal son. But to give God control of her life…when she'd worked so hard to become strong and self-sufficient…was a different matter.

Maybe she'd never be ready for, or capable of, that kind of trust. The thought disturbed her, and she banged the bread pan down on the countertop harder than she'd expected. It was frustrating to face the truth, though. Cassie felt that she'd come home to God already. But to turn over every part of her life to him? It seemed impossible.

Of course, a long-term relationship with Lee, or anyone else, felt pretty impossible, too. It might be more likely if Lee's expectations of marriage were different from what she was used to. Lee, she suspected, would go into marriage knowing that this was his partner for life. Both their lives, long and whole, not broken up by other people or other problems. It was the only way Cassie would ever go into marriage again. If she ever did.

Sitting here in her kitchen late at night, most of the Thanksgiving dinner preparations underway, she had to admit two things. She was falling in love with Lee Winter. And she was terrified of the prospect of what that love might bring.

Morning brought all the happy confusion of a holiday. The kids enjoyed the "no school" aspect of the day first, hanging around in their pajamas and getting out projects to fill Cassie's clean living room. Since she had expected nothing less, she wasn't disturbed. "As long as everything is picked up by noon and you're dressed like normal human beings, you have the morning off," she told them both.

They might have the morning off, but she didn't. What she was doing was actually labor she enjoyed, though. She baked the loaf of bread that had risen during the night, and once it was done, the turkey was ready to go into the oven so it could be cooling, waiting to carve when Lee came. It looked awfully big for four people. Even four people and a puppy, assuming he'd get a little scrap or two, Cassie thought. Still, everybody liked turkey sandwiches and the like, so she wouldn't be upset to have leftovers.

Cassie cleaned fresh green beans and got them ready to cook later, then she got out a real cloth tablecloth and set the table as fancy as she possibly could. She had bright red cloth napkins, a wedding present that hid in the linen closet most days. She looked at them, marveling at their wonderful texture and wondered again why she made do with paper most of the time.

Even her everyday dishes and glassware looked special on a nicely set table. She decorated a basket with pine cones and some red and gold leaves the kids had collected on walks in the park, then added a couple gourds and baby pumpkins. For the final touch, she surrounded the centerpiece with fat red candles. It was a nearly perfect table.

She still felt a little odd about setting the table for four instead of three. Not uncomfortable, just different. It was nice to have a man around the house, she had to admit. Maybe the blades to the ceiling fan would actually get cleaned before Christmas without her climbing on a stepladder, she mused. Stepping back, she admired her table setting. "Pretty good job, if I do say so myself," Cassie murmured to no one in particular, the children still busy with their craft work in the living room.

She gave everything a last check, and satisfied, she went to shower and dress herself. Lunch would be a simple sandwich eaten in the living room on paper plates. Maybe she could even talk Sarah into making peanut butter double deckers for everybody. It would make everybody feel good—Cassie and Zach because they both liked peanut butter sandwiches, and Sarah because she could then say she fixed lunch.

As it turned out, it worked just that way. They sat around the coffee table, divested now of all its craft items, and ate and talked. "Be thinking of something to say at the dinner table later," Cassie warned them. "I want everybody to tell something they're thankful for."

Zach nodded, his mouth full of peanut butter. "Cool," he said, once he swallowed. Cassie hoped he'd remember that little rule when Lee was present. "I can do that. There's a ton of things I'm thankful for this year."

"Me, too," Sarah admitted. "I'm thankful I'm not the shortest kid in my class, I'm thankful I get to go to my own school next year...."

"How about some positive things," her mother urged.

Sarah grinned, aware her teasing had gotten to her mother. "I guess I can think of one of those, too, if you want."

"I want," Cassie told her. She was growing up so fast. She

was already testing the limits when she could, preparing for that teenage firestorm Cassie was sure would come soon. But Sarah was a good kid, and a bright one, and they'd get through it all together.

There were times when she was almost glad Brad wasn't around. He had been an indulgent father in the worst ways, unable or unwilling to back her up on discipline or rules. He hated to say no to his children, and as a result, Cassie always felt uncomfortable leaving him alone with them for very long because of what she'd find when she got back. A half hour trip to the grocery store had usually meant a scene of total chaos when she came home.

She knew Sarah was at the age where structure and rules, no matter how much she protested against them, were just what she needed. And she also knew that Lee, if he stuck around, would help provide those things. Still, she hated to get too dependent on that. If Sarah got too attached to Lee and then he didn't end up staying, it would be hard to explain to a vulnerable preteen. Finishing her sandwich, Cassie pushed her worries away. She had a turkey to check on and other little chores to do. Worrying about the future could wait.

As it was, her chores kept her busy enough that she didn't have any time to worry the rest of the day before the doorbell rang at four. She could hear Skippy yapping in the background and Lee's deep laugh as he spoke to the little dog on the other side of the door. "Yeah, you know where you are, all right."

When she opened the door, the puppy sprang in. He was growing faster than Sarah, taking on the size and shape of an adult dog more every week. Today he was just gorgeous; brushed until he shone and with the red bow that Lee had promised tied around his neck.

"You managed to do it," she said. "Come in. I don't know which one of you guys looks the best, but I'm happy to see you both." While Lee came in and got Zach to hang up his jacket, Cassie cooed over the puppy who danced around her legs, begging for attention. She made him sit first, then petted and praised him for doing so, while his brown tail thumped on the carpet. Looking up at Lee, she smiled. "You are doing such a nice job with him."

"Now that the cast is off, he's easier to train. And he was a good little dog to begin with," Lee said. "Happy Thanksgiving."

"And the same to you," Cassie told him, walking into the hug he offered. His bright red sweater looked terribly festive. She marveled again at how handsome Lee was, in or out of uniform. His cologne teased her nose with a woodsy scent in their quick hug, and then he stepped back, with his hand out.

"I brought a box of chocolates. For after dinner, of course. But it's a holiday, and my mom would skin me if she thought I'd gone someplace without a 'hostess gift' as she'd call it."

"I want to meet this lady," Cassie said with a laugh, taking the proffered box of goodies. "She obviously raised all of you right."

"That she did. Of course Dad helped a lot. But the manners thing seemed to be Mom's department."

"Well, tell her for me that she succeeded, the next time you talk to her," Cassie said. "How much time do you want to unwind before you cut the turkey?"

"How long has it been out of the oven?" Lee countered. "It smells great in here. If the bird's been cooking long enough, let me shuck this sweater, roll up my sleeves, and get at it. After, of course, I perform one vital step."

"And what would that be?" Cassie asked, following him into the kitchen.

"Sampling the skin. You guys do eat the turkey skin, don't you?"

Cassie wrinkled her nose. "No. Usually I pull it off before I slice it. You eat that stuff?"

Lee nodded. "So does the rest of the family. There's a virtual stampede into the kitchen when the call for turkey skin goes out. Boy, if you don't eat turkey skin, I really will have to bring you home to Mother. She'll be so glad to have an ally, she won't know what to do."

Cassie laughed, watching him survey her carving knives and the turkey. "Well, eat as much as you like of the silly stuff because nobody else will touch it."

"Hey, you hear that, Skippy? The lady is telling me to eat all the turkey skin I want. She doesn't know me very well, does she?" Lee said with a grin. "Wait until I call my sister. She'll be so jealous. There'll be at least seven of them down there in Mobile wrangling over that skin."

Cassie shook her head. Maybe she didn't know Lee very well. But this getting to know him was fun. While he pulled bits of crispy skin off the turkey, muttering to himself in happiness, she got things ready to make the gravy. This was a real Thanksgiving, one with so many things to be incredibly thankful for. And right now, the thing she was most thankful for was this good man and his delight over such a simple gift. He acted as if he'd been given diamonds, not a patch of browned turkey. Stirring broth and drippings in a pan, Cassie giggled. Thankful for turkey skin! What would Lee teach her next?

Ten

*L*ee Winter looked around. He was one contented guy. Even if he couldn't go home for Thanksgiving, somehow a little corner of home had come to him. Here he sat, just finishing a marvelous turkey dinner, complete with more turkey skin than he could possibly eat, even with a dog to share it.

Said dog sat happily in the corner of the kitchen on what Cassie called his favorite rug. How a dog had favorite anythings, except maybe sticks and people, Lee wasn't sure. But he humored her on that one, and she might have been right; Skippy now headed for that particular spot whenever he wanted a good snooze. At the moment, he had given up napping to chew on the rawhide knot that Cassie and the kids had gotten him as part of his own personal Thanksgiving feast. They spoiled his dog horribly, and he loved every minute of it. Lee couldn't object to it much himself.

Cassie and the kids spoiled him almost as much as they did the dog. He had a warm house to go to, with friendly people in it, whenever his own place got too quiet or empty. Zach adored shooting baskets with him outside at the hoop when it was warm enough, or beating him at board games when it was too cold to go out.

Sarah actually asked his opinion on things she considered important and took his suggestions. Of course, it probably helped that he was an interested adult who wasn't her parent. She was getting to the age where everybody needed a few friends who were definitely not their parents, Lee thought. He felt honored that he got to be one of Sarah's.

And then there was Cassie. She was so lovely. So warm and friendly, and so excited by her work at the school. If there was only some way he could help her get that degree. She would make the most wonderful teacher. But Lee knew just enough about her to know that Cassie's pride wouldn't take that kind of help from anybody, not even him.

What he really wanted to do was make a tiny chink in that pride. Not for him to come through, but for the Lord to step in. All he needed was the tiniest parting of her armor. It was hard to convince somebody as independent as Cassie that dependence on anybody, even God, was a good idea. He'd just have to keep praying and quietly pointing things out and hope that Cassie found her way to all the wonders God had stored up for her, if she'd just open her hands for them.

She was so hungry for it all. Lee marveled at the way she soaked up everything, from Scripture reading when she turned her mind to it, to the simplest little things. She said grace with the children at meals now, even when he wasn't here. And she'd started taking them to church and Sunday school at his church. Not that it had to be there, as far as he was concerned. But it was a thrill to see her there every week.

The puppy was back to sleeping on his rug, part of his rawhide knot squirreled away under one paw for later. The kids had finished eating and were getting antsy about being at the table. Lee decided it was time for a little conversation. "So, if this is Thanksgiving, who's thankful for something?" he asked.

He wasn't prepared for the laughter that welled up in the three of them. It wasn't unkind laughter, rather a joyous shout. "Mom was right!" Zach crowed. "She said you *might* get through dinner before you asked. I've been thinking of stuff all afternoon."

The dog had popped off his rug at the noise and was standing next to Zach, bounding up on his knee. The boy pushed him down gently. "Not at the table, Skip," he told him, mindful of Lee's rules. It gave Lee a swell of pleasure that the boy was willing to help train the little dog the way he wanted him trained. "Mine's easy. Skippy, definitely. And you, too, Lee. I'm thankful for you." His shining face was so innocent and honest that Lee felt a sweet ache in his chest, looking at him.

"Aw, you took mine. But not in that order," Sarah said. Around her family she didn't have quite the shy, guarded front she had at school. She didn't have to worry here about being cool and smart and saying exactly the right thing. Here she could be a kid most of the time and enjoy it. She jumped out of her chair and ran around the table to Lee. "I'm thankful for you, too." She gave him a quick hug before she bounced back to her seat.

Cassie's eyes glistened. *Aren't they wonderful?* her silent expression seemed to ask. Lee wanted to tell her that of course her children were wonderful. She had raised them. How could they be any other way?

Instead, he just looked at her and smiled. She smiled back, a little watery, but a definite smile. "They stole my thunder, for sure. I'm so thankful for you, Lee. And all the good you've brought into our lives. Not just Skippy, although you are cute," she told the pup, who'd come up to her all wiggly when he heard his name. "I'm especially thankful that you've brought us back home."

"We weren't away from home, Mom," Zach said. "Except for you, the other night when your car got smashed. I'm thankful for that, too. Not it getting smashed, but that you didn't get smashed with it."

"Oh, Zachary, so am I. Very, very thankful. But we were away from home," his mother said gently. "Not this home, with four walls. But God's home that he has waiting for all of us. And I hadn't had my face pointed toward that home for a long time. Not until Lee got me headed in the right direction. That's what I'm thankful about."

Lee smiled, unable to say anything for a moment. Things were going to be all right between him and Cassie, he knew then. Even if nothing ever went any farther between them than it already had, he knew why he'd been introduced into her life. And again, he thought, he was a very contented man. Contented and very thankful.

Surely it was time to celebrate some of those feelings. "I'm thankful for all of you, too," he said. "Without you to help me, I couldn't have Skippy. And I've really wanted my own dog for a while. I've rescued plenty of them, just the way I did him, but I always had to give them to somebody else."

"Aw…" Zach said in sympathy. He seemed to understand what it was to want something you couldn't quite have. Lee wondered how many things there were like that in his life. Chief among them was probably a father.

"And I'm thankful for the three of you for other reasons, too, not just because you watch Skippy," Lee said. "I'm especially thankful that you guys are such generous, resourceful kids who found a way for me to ask your mom out on a date."

The kids giggled, and Cassie blushed. "I think I want to get up and clear the table," she said, looking flustered.

"Let's all help," Lee said, getting up himself. "If I don't get up soon, I may not be able to do it at all."

Standing and stretching felt great. A nap on the couch in the living room would feel pretty good, too, and he felt comfortable enough around all of these people to do just that. But he had a few things to do first.

He helped clear the table, and once that was done and Cassie was putting away leftovers and the kids were loading the dishwasher, he leaned against the kitchen cabinets, watching. "You know, I think it's about time for another date," he said. "Only this time, I think it ought to be my turn to do the picking, choosing, and paying."

"That sounds good to me," Cassie said with a smile. Lee was surprised she hadn't put up an argument. She would later, when he told her that he intended to pay Sarah for watching her brother, as well as taking Cassie out to dinner. But he'd save that argument for later, or maybe find some way to sidestep it all together.

"How 'bout Saturday night?" Lee asked. "Or do you have big plans for the weekend already?"

"Not really. I might do a little Christmas shopping, if I can slip away," Cassie said, smiling as broadly as the kids. "But otherwise, I'm free."

"That's good to hear. We'll work out the time and place later," Lee said. "Maybe while we're doing the pots and pans that don't fit into the dishwasher."

Cassie waved him away. "I hadn't intended for you to help with that."

"I want to," Lee said. "I didn't do anything towards cooking this wonderful meal, or cleaning the house, or all the other things that had to happen for today to take place. Surely I could help with the dishes."

"If you really want to," Cassie said, her expression showing what a foreign idea this was to her.

"I want to," Lee assured her, wishing again that he could get her to talk about Bradley. Just once. Just for a little while, so that he could find out what that man must have done, or not done, to make this beautiful woman so wary. Whatever it was, he felt as if it might take his entire lifetime to convince Cassie that whatever kind of man her husband had been, he wasn't that same kind.

Saturday night he slipped Sarah a phone number and address. "This is where we'll be. Don't show Mom, okay?" he said, with a conspiratorial wink, which Sarah returned.

Cassie grimaced slightly. "I don't know if I like this. What if I'm not dressed right?"

Lee looked her over. The dark slacks and bright sweater looked great to him, and he said so. "As long as you have on clean socks under those boots, you'll be fine," he said, trying not to crack a grin.

"Clean socks?" her voice rose at least half an octave. "Wherever are you taking me?"

"Well, it could be that Japanese place, where you have to leave your shoes at the door. And I figure you might want clean socks. You *do* like eel, don't you?"

The expression on Cassie's face was too good. He couldn't help laughing. She came over and punched him on the arm, more gently than he would someone who'd been yanking his chain this hard. "I should know better than to even ask by now," she said. "You're truly irrepressible, do you know that?"

"I live for it," Lee admitted.

"Good. We're not really having eel someplace, are we? Because I've never tried it, and I do urge the kids to be adventurous, but I don't think I could be a good example and eat eel," she said, wrinkling her adorable nose just a bit.

"Tastes just like chicken," Lee said, trying to keep his poker face again. "But no, we're not having eel. And you don't really need the clean socks. Although they would make a lovely addition to any outfit."

Cassie sighed. "Oh, let's go before I have to listen to any more of this." She seemed to be enjoying it, though, even as she protested. It was one of the reasons Lee liked being with her. She gave as good as she got, a valuable quality when dealing with somebody who had been shaped by police work for the better part of a decade the way he had. He suspected any woman in his life for long would have to have a strong personality to survive. In most respects, Cassie certainly fit the bill.

Watching her watch him drive and try to guess where they were going was fun. He purposefully took a route to the restaurant which led them past several other places, just to watch her peer out the window and guess. Finally, he circled around and pulled into the parking lot of a strip mall not more than two miles from Cassie's house, and scarcely more from his.

"Oh, really? I've always wanted to try this place," Cassie said, looking at the sign over the door. "But I wasn't sure they'd have anything the kids would like."

"You'll love it," Lee assured her, walking into his favorite Italian restaurant with his favorite lady on his arm. It was time to introduce them to each other.

While they were waiting for appetizers, Lee gave Cassie as much history as he could about DiMarcos—how the owner and his daughters had come over from Sicily a few years before, settling in an area already ripe with restaurants but still managing to carve out a delightful niche for themselves anyway.

He'd been one of their first customers their first week open, and he and Frank had shared a few cups of espresso at odd hours since then as the business grew. "I really like the place," he told Cassie. "It's homey and classy at the same time."

She looked around thoughtfully and nodded. "I see what

you mean. And having real napkins and linen tablecloths is so nice. It's a change from the places we usually frequent, where most of the food comes on a tray wrapped in paper."

"Well, that's life with kids," he said. "That reminds me that the DARE program benefit at McDonalds is next weekend. Wanna come watch me serve drinks?"

Cassie smiled. "Sure. I'll bet you're great at it."

"Yeah, well, it's the most challenging thing they let me do. One year they put me in charge of fries and I nearly burnt the place down, so now all I do is shovel ice and pour cola," he said, enjoying her laughter.

"I don't believe a word of it," she told him, reaching across the table for his hand. "But it's entertaining to hear it from you just the same."

They had a wonderful dinner. Afterwards, Lee couldn't have told anyone just what it was he ate. It hadn't been the food that made the dinner so good. It had been Cassie's company, and the way that the DiMarco girls seemed to know that something was up, as they kept coming out of the kitchen to refresh his and Cassie's ice waters and to make sure they had enough bread, the whole works.

It was the middle one, Francesca, who came to the table just about the time Lee was ready to order coffee. "You are Mrs. Neel?" she asked Cassie. "You have a phone call."

Cassie sprang from the table, laughter erased from her face in an instant. When she came back a moment later, Lee knew by her pale complexion and set expression that it was time to roll. "It was Sarah," she said. "Zach hurt himself. I think we're going to the emergency room."

Lee nodded, standing up and getting his wallet. He put money on the table, more than he knew would cover the bill. "We've got to go now," he told Francesca. "I'll come back for my change sometime." She nodded. It wouldn't be the first time something had pulled Lee out of a restaurant before he'd finished his meal. But because it was someone he cared about, this time his heart was pounding like a bass drum as he ushered Cassie out into the cold darkness.

Eleven

*L*ee drove the way Cassie suspected police officers normally drove on the way to the hospital. Normally when she was with him she was impressed with his smooth, easy handling of his Jeep. Tonight everything was turned up a few degrees.

Sarah sat in the front seat with him. She was crying again. "I didn't know, Mom," she said. "I really didn't know. He told me he could do it himself, so I let him."

"And that would have been fine if I'd been there, Sarah," her mother said softly, with one hand still on Zach's shoulder. "You couldn't have known that this was going to happen."

"It's not Sarah's fault," Zach said. "I talked her into this."

"I'm sure you did, Zachary," Cassie said. "We'll be there in a minute."

Tears ran down his face as well, but unlike Sarah, they weren't tears of fear and contrition, just pure pain. Cassie tried to quell the panic rising in her. What if he'd done permanent damage to his eyes with something as silly as a bag of microwave popcorn? Whether the damage was permanent or not, her baby was hurt. And she felt so bad for leaving him, for letting it happen in the first place.

"Go on in with him and I'll park and meet you," Lee said, stopping at the door of the emergency room. Cassie nodded and slid out of the car, ushering Zach through the whoosh of the opening doors.

They spent a moment at a desk, where a young woman took all the pertinent information and had just settled into seats in the waiting room when Lee and Sarah came in.

When the triage nurse came from the back room and saw Lee in the waiting room, she came up to him. *He probably knows everybody in here,* Cassie thought, wondering if that was a good thing or not. "No, just friend of the family," she heard Lee telling the nurse. "But it would be great if you could get him back there soon. I know he's really hurting."

Zach was squirming in his chair, not quite to the point of having a bawling fit. Cassie could feel in his tensed muscles what it was costing him to stay as still as he was. "You're doing a great job," she told him. "And you heard Lee. They'll see you in a few minutes."

"But it hurts!" Zach wailed, finally close to the breaking point.

"And I'll bet you're scared," Lee said, on his knees before the boy, one arm around him. "I would be. I've been in here for stuff before, and if it's me doing the waiting, it's always painful and scary. One time I went over a fence after a guy and had to get six stitches. Right where I jumped over the fence," he said, leaning over to whisper in Zach's ear just exactly where those stitches had been, Cassie guessed. Whatever he said, it brought a fleeting smile to Zach's face.

"How about saying a quick prayer together, Zach?" Lee asked, more serious now. "You know, Jesus is always with you, even when you're hurt and scared. Let's ask him to let you be real aware of him being with you. Maybe it will make things a little easier."

Zach nodded, and Lee engulfed his hands, which looked so small to Cassie right now, in his bigger ones. He prayed, quietly and earnestly with the boy, who got out a few words between gulps of calming his sobs. They'd just said "amen" together when the triage nurse was back.

"Zachary Neel," she called. "Come with me. Mom, you come too," she said. "Is there somebody to stay with your sister?"

Zach nodded. "Lee's here. We'll be okay." When he squared his shoulders as he stood and said it, Cassie believed it herself for the first time in an hour. Maybe they would all be okay tonight.

"Well, Zachary, what have you done to yourself?" the doctor said a few minutes later, pausing at the doorway to their cubicle. She was a slight woman with glossy black hair and delicate hands, and Cassie felt thankful for her gentle manner. Those hands were deft as well as gentle as she began examining Zach while he told her about the accident.

"I hadn't ever fixed my own popcorn before, but I told Sarah I could and she let me. When the microwave stopped, it didn't feel like it was done, so I put it back in there. And once I started it again it started making funny noises, and it smelled bad, so I stopped it, and I took it out, and I shook it a little bit, and then I opened it real quick."

"And all that hot stuff came out in your face and it hurt," the doctor said succinctly. "Anything else?"

Zach nodded, eyes still clenched shut. "Some of the popcorn wasn't done popping yet, and it exploded when I opened the bag. It hit me in the eye. And now my eye hurts."

The doctor went over to the shelves of equipment and supplies and got a packet. "This has a sterile towelette in it. I'm going to open it and wipe your face around that eye. It will feel cool, and a little wet, but it shouldn't sting anymore than it does already. And I bet it really does sting, doesn't it?"

Zach nodded. "Now if you can be brave for me and let me open that eye and take a quick look, I may not have to do much more that will hurt. You want Mom to hold your hand?"

"Yeah." The doctor patted his shoulder.

"Okay. Then Mom, come over here and do the hand holding. Don't be surprised if he squeezes pretty hard. He looks strong to me."

"Oh, he is," Cassie said, going along with the doctor's distraction of her son. It didn't take her long to wipe off his face and gently open his eyelid and assess the eye.

"Okay. Now if you want to stretch out on that table for a couple minutes, you can. I need to get another doctor in here to look and see if he thinks the same thing I do. If he does, we'll do a couple things, and you'll be on your way."

Zach laid back on the table and let go of Cassie's hand. "Don't rub that eye any, no matter how much you want to," the doctor cautioned him. She motioned Cassie close to the doorway of the cubicle. "No permanent damage. If there was, we'd see a whole lot more trauma."

"So he didn't…"

"Blind himself?" the doctor finished very quietly. "No, not at all. He's not going to be very comfortable for a couple days. But no, he's not going to be blind, either."

Cassie felt herself sag a little in relief. "You okay, Mom?" the doctor said, squeezing her shoulder. "I've got three of my own. I recognize the signs of mother fatigue here. Don't pass out on me, okay?"

"Okay," Cassie said, trying to smile through her shakes. The doctor disappeared for a few moments and came back with a colleague, who looked in Zach's eyes, and the two doctors talked for a while. Cassie was able to catch fragments of their conversation, but it wasn't in terms she could always understand.

Finally they both left, then the pediatrician came back by herself. "Okay, Zachary, here's the deal," she said, putting a hand on his blue jean covered knee. "You have probably scratched your cornea with that popcorn. That's the clear window part of your eye, and it heals really fast if we help it. That's the good news."

"What's the bad news?" Zach asked, seeming to know there was some just from the doctor's manner.

"Between the scratch and the fact that Dr. Robb and I both think you have a little steam scald there, too, you're going to have to play pirate for a couple days and wear a patch. We're going to put some gummy yellow ointment in there, then tape on the patch. You have to keep it on, no matter what, and let your mom change it twice a day, okay?"

Zach slumped back on the table. "Okay, I guess. Will it stop hurting?"

"Mostly," the doctor said. "Keeping it shut with the patch on will help the hurt more than anything because it will stop the movement of that eye most of the time. When it doesn't move, nothing will rub on that scratch and make it sting."

A nurse came in with a basin and more supplies, and she and the doctor went to work quickly treating and bandaging Zach's eye. While they worked, the doctor gave Cassie instructions on how to change the bandage herself. "He needs to see an ophthalmologist in about forty-eight hours. Things should have mostly healed by then, if he's on track. Stop by the desk and they will give you the card of the group we recommend for kids, okay?"

"Fine. It's amazing," Cassie said, "that something this serious will heal in a couple days."

"The human body is pretty amazing all around when you think about it," the doctor said. She stopped what she was doing and smiled gently at Cassie. "And how long will it take for you to heal? I think we have two patients here. One who tried to be a little too independent for his own good, and one who is beating herself up for letting him do that."

"Three if you count my daughter in the waiting room," Cassie admitted. "In fact, I need to go out and tell her that things are okay."

"Do that," the doctor said. "And start believing it yourself."

"I will," Cassie promised. "I will."

It got easier by the minute to believe. Sarah looked so relieved Cassie thought she might slide out of her chair. "He's not hurt bad? I was so scared I let him do something that was going to really hurt him. But, Mom, he said he was old enough, and I thought he probably was, and…"

"That part we can talk about later," Cassie told her, giving her a hug. "For now he's going to be all right. He's going to look a little odd for a couple days, and I certainly don't want any teasing."

"Don't worry," Sarah said, looking somber. "I wouldn't tease him about this for anything. And I'll deck anybody at school who does."

"Well, you don't have to deck them. Just warn them off, okay?" Cassie said, surprised at the vehemence with which Sarah was ready to defend her little brother. "Now I've got to go back in there with him."

By the time she got back to the cubicle, Zach was nearly ready to go. The patch didn't look very threatening. It was just a square of gauze and tape covering one eye. Zach looked tired and ready to go home, and Cassie was happy to lead him out of the emergency room. Lee and Sarah brought the car around while she got last minute instructions on treatment, the eye doctor's card, and prescriptions to fill at the pharmacy for more ointment and pain medication if needed. "And remember what I said," the pediatrician told her. "Don't keep telling yourself this was all your fault. Kids do things like this every day. Believe me, I see them all."

"I'm sure," Cassie said. But in her heart of hearts she had to admit that she felt terribly responsible. She was thankful it hadn't turned out worse. Worse, she told herself, was probably what she deserved for leaving her baby just to have a good time.

Twelve

I t was another hour before everybody got back to Cassie's and got settled. "I'm staying the night. No arguments," Lee said. By then it was nearly midnight, and Cassie didn't feel like arguing with anybody. "You're going to need help with Zach, and you all need sleep."

"Fine. You're right," Cassie said, although she wasn't sure it was fine and was even less sure that Lee was right. All she knew was that *she* wasn't feeling fine at all, and she did need the help, so it was easier to agree with him than to argue. If she started to disagree right now she could see the discussion quickly degenerating into something like the second graders got into at recess.

"You go get Sarah settled and Zach can show me where the sleeping bags are," Lee told her. "We'll be camped out in the living room if you need us."

"I'll be there soon," Cassie said, trying to find the energy to drag her body down the hall to Sarah's room. "Once you get the sleeping bags set up, make sure he takes one of his pain pills."

"Will do," Lee said. "Then maybe we can get some sleep, huh, Zach?"

"Yeah," Zach said. He looked like a beaten prizefighter, weaving slightly on his feet. "Sleeping bags are in my closet. Up at the top."

"I'll get them. That's what I'm here for," Cassie heard Lee say as they went down to the end of the hall. By then she was at Sarah's room, and she knocked on the closed door. Closed doors and knocking had gotten very important in the last few months, and she figured tonight would be no exception.

Sarah's "Come in," was muffled. When Cassie entered the room, she saw her daughter sprawled out on the bed, on top of the comforter, still dressed. She had tears on her face again.

"What's the matter, Sarah?" Cassie asked, going to her side.

"Oh, Mommy, I was so scared." It wasn't the tears as much as Sarah reverting to the name she hadn't called her in years that made Cassie kneel by the bed and scoop up her daughter to let her cry in her arms while she hugged her.

She smelled of shampoo and warm child, and Cassie snuggled her into her arms. "It wasn't your fault, sweetie. It really wasn't."

"But I shouldn't have let him use the microwave by himself. You don't let him," Sarah said, gulping between sobs. "He hurt himself. Bad."

"Yes, he did. Not so terribly bad as we thought at first. And you did the right thing calling next door then calling me at the restaurant. All in all, I'd say you made the best of a bad situation."

Sarah shook her head, still buried in her mother's shoulder. "No, I didn't. You probably don't ever want me to watch him again."

"Oh, Sarah, no. You'll get a chance again, I promise. Maybe not for a little while," Cassie admitted, taking a deep breath herself. "Because I feel like this is all my fault for leaving the two of you, not yours for being in charge."

Sarah's eyes were wide, ringed with damp lashes. "But Mom, I asked and asked to be allowed to be in charge. And I did all right before, every time. Everybody goes places by themselves sometimes. You should get to go out without us sometimes, too."

"I guess so. But I know if I'd been here this wouldn't have happened," Cassie said.

"Maybe not," Sarah said. "But I bet Zach could have found some other way to do something like that. Remember that time when he was four, and he and Robbie decided to see who could jump the highest, and Robbie was wearing ski boots and Zach was in his socks.…"

"All too well," Cassie said, reflecting on emergency rooms past. "You may have a point there, Sarah. I'll make you a deal. I won't blame myself more than nine or ten more times for this if you won't blame yourself either."

She got a shaky grin through the last of the tears. "Deal, Mom." Sarah hugged her back, fiercely.

"Now let's tuck you in," she said. "And then I have to go join the camp out in the living room."

Sarah wrinkled her nose. "This is one camp out I'm glad I'm not a part of."

Cassie had to admit to herself she felt the same way. She felt tired and drained already, and the thought of the challenges of watching a fretful child through the night sounded painful. Still, she went to her bedroom and changed into old sweats and went back to the living room where Zach was settled into a sleeping bag already, and Lee was telling him a story.

He looked more like a neglected stuffed animal than a pirate, with the patch surrounded by blond curls. "Night, Mom," he said sleepily. "Lee's telling me about three guys who didn't get burned up."

"They didn't, huh?" Cassie said, remembering the story of

Shadrach, Meshach, and Abednego. She smiled as she bent to kiss him on the forehead, away from the bandage. "We'll be here all night. Wake us up if you have any problems, okay?"

"Okay. Right now it doesn't hurt too much. It feels kind of weird, but it doesn't hurt," Zach said, yawning again. He turned back to Lee, stretched out on a sleeping bag nearby. "Go ahead. What happened after the king threw them into the furnace?"

Lee, talking softly, finished the story while Cassie stretched out on the couch, with Zach between herself and Lee. It had been a while since she'd heard the story of Shadrach, Meshach, and Abednego, and she was sure that Zach had never heard it. And Lee, with his flair for drama and adventure, managed to tell it just right. Zach dozed off into a satisfied-looking sleep as Lee finished the story.

"That should hold him awhile," he said softly, looking over at Cassie. "Try to get some rest, and I'll take the first shift."

"Sure. But why do you think he needs watching? Is there something I didn't understand about this at the emergency room?" Cassie asked, feeling a little worried. "Is he in some kind of danger?"

"No, not danger," Lee said. "But I've seen people bandaged up like this before. The body's first response, once it gets into deep sleep, is to remove anything that disturbs it. He's going to do a lot better if he doesn't rub that spot, or try to take off the bandage."

"He won't do that, will he? Sound asleep?" Cassie asked.

"Watch," Lee said, getting up off his sleeping bag and turning off the lamps until only a pale glow from the kitchen gave any illumination to the room. Everything was quiet for a few moments. Then Zach turned slightly in his sleep, and the fabric of the sleeping bag rustled. One arm slid out of the bag and up toward his face. Quickly but gently, Lee guided it down, away from the bandage. Zach muttered a little but didn't wake fully.

"Come on, Zach. Just relax and let that be," he told the sleeping boy.

Cassie watched the two of them. "I guess you're right. I'll let you take the first shift it you want it. Wake me up in an hour. Sooner if you get tired."

"Will do," Lee said, sliding Zach's arm back into the sleeping bag. For a moment, Cassie just watched the two of them and felt the most enormous rush of love for this man. On that thought, she let her tired body take the rest it had been pleading for during the long evening in the emergency room. As she dozed off, she could hear the two of them in what she suspected would be the rhythm of the hour; Zach's arm moving over the slippery fabric of the bag, and Lee's calm voice. "Not this time, son. Let's go back to sleep."

4:00 A.M. Cassie's least favorite hour in the twenty-four that made up a day. It was too early to be morning and too late to be night. And in her experience, nothing good ever happened then anyway. The only good 4:00 A.M.'s she'd ever known were those she slept through. If she was awake, it was not a good sign.

After Brad died, she found herself awake at that time of the morning quite often. It was the time that she jolted awake, sure she'd heard a crying child, only to discover it had been nothing but her own bad dreams or troubled thoughts that awakened her. Then she'd stay awake, tangled in the sheets and worrying about her future, until daybreak.

Tonight wasn't much different from those bad old days or nights. She and Lee had been up and down with Zach countless times. He didn't come to complete wakefulness often. When he did, it was with pain and aggravation. At about three he was wide awake and near tears. "It hurts. And it itches. And

I can't go to school Monday because I'll look like a dork," he cried.

"I'm sorry it hurts. And I'm sure it itches, too. And we'll worry about school later," Cassie told him. "How about if I rub your back?"

"No!" Zach roared. "I don't want anybody to touch me. I just want it to stop hurting. And itching."

"Calm down, Zach," Lee said, roused out of what little sleep he'd gotten. "If you get too excited and hot, you're going to start sweating under that bandage. And it's going to be even more itchy than it is now, and there'd be salty old sweat under there. You don't want that, do you?"

"No. I don't." Zach sounded so small. Cassie wished there was something she could do.

"Do you want another one of the pain pills? You could have one with some cold water, if you like." It was past the time the doctor had said he would be allowed one, and although Cassie hated to give him anything, she could tell that he hurt. And they seemed to make him drowsy as well.

"Maybe," Zach said. "They sure are bigger than those cold things I usually swallow."

"Yeah, but they're slippery. That's because they're coated with gelatin," Lee said. "Bet you don't know where that stuff comes from."

Cassie could hear Zach's "No way," as she went to the kitchen to run the coldest water possible and get Zach a pill. He took it without much problem, pausing to tell her the grue-some details of gelatin, à la Lee Winter. Afterwards, he settled back down in his sleeping bag and dozed off again. She, how-ever, was awake, of course. It was 4:00 A.M.

"Can't sleep either?" Lee whispered across Zach.

"No," Cassie said. "I didn't mean to wake you, though."

"You didn't. I was awake on my own," Lee told her. "Let's go in the kitchen and sit up for a while. I think he's sound enough asleep he's not going to bother the bandage for a while."

Cassie rose from the couch and followed him into the kitchen. The single bulb over the stove was the only illumination. Outside there was little moon, no stars. She felt so tired and downhearted.

"Is it always like this?" Lee said, sounding as tired as she felt. "Having a sick kid, or a hurt kid, I mean. I hurt for him."

Cassie nodded. "You don't have to. I'm doing plenty of it for both of us."

"Yeah, but you're used to it. I've never felt like this before. I mean, I've helped the paramedics take kids to the ER before, if there were people who didn't really need an ambulance or something. And I've dealt with lost kids, and kids in DARE with problems. But I could always step back a little and detach myself. I can't do that with Zach."

"You're doing a good job with him," Cassie said. *Better than his own father would have done,* she added silently. "And I'm sorry you're getting too close."

"Am I? Too close, Cassie?" Lee sounded angry. "I don't feel too close. I feel barely close enough. You don't let anybody get very close."

"See what happens when I do," she shot back. "This is the closest I've let anybody get in years. And it hasn't been pretty. Since we've gotten this close, I've been confused most of the time. You've brought me back to church and got me thinking about God, but where is that leading? I've been in a car wreck that totaled my car, and my son nearly put his eye out tonight. What is God trying to tell me?"

Lee looked like she'd punched him in the stomach. After a moment, he sat down at the kitchen table and motioned her to do the same. Pushing her hair out of her eyes, and fighting tears, she joined him. Lee took her hand, and she was struck again by how warm he was. How caring and reassuring, even when she had just lashed out at him.

"First of all, God loves you and counts you as his special child, Cassie. No matter what part I play in your life from now on, God is still going to be there. He's been there even when you turned your back on him. Maybe I did lead you back to him. If so, I'm honored that I could do that for somebody. But you belong to him, Cassie. And only you and he can sort out the relationship you need to have with him."

All the while he talked, Lee looked at her, blue eyes steady and unblinking. Cassie felt her heart slow and her breathing even out as he spoke. "You're right, Lee," she said softly. "I'm sorry for lashing out at you that way. But it's so easy to think that God must be punishing me with all this rotten stuff that's happening to me. I mean, I was away from him so long."

"That's the beauty of Jesus, Cassie. He took on all our troubles, pain, and suffering. All our sin. All we have to do is believe in him. God's not up there somewhere keeping score, saying, 'I think I'll make Cassie Neel's life miserable because she ignored me for a while.' Instead, there's Jesus, who would rather go out looking for the one lost sheep than count ninety-nine of them that are already safe in the fold."

"At least I don't feel lost anymore," Cassie said, looking down at the table. She felt so bad for striking out at Lee. "Just awfully confused."

"Well, join the crowd, Cass," Lee said, squeezing her hands. "I feel confused a lot, too. God doesn't ever say that we'll understand everything. Not here on earth, anyway." He paused and sighed thoughtfully. "I'm really going to have to introduce you to Miss Dorothy. Maybe if Zach's up to church later this morning, we can do that."

"Maybe," Cassie said weakly, thinking that it was highly unlikely that Zachary would be going anywhere that day. "Now if you still feel like talking, let's go back to something else you said there. About what direction our relationship is going to take in the future. Want to talk about that?" Cassie thought she'd found the ticket to going back to sleep. What man was going to talk about commitment, especially at this hour?

Lee's forthright answer surprised her a little. His mouth turned up at one corner in half a smile. "Suddenly I'm all talked out. And maybe not as ready to forge full steam ahead here as I thought. Do you really want to do this at four in the morning?"

Cassie chuckled softly. His grin had softened her heart, and his answer had touched her more deeply than flowery words could have. "Not really. I think I know enough already, Lee. Any guy that's willing to stay up all night with someone else's sick child is saying something by his actions. You don't need words, and certainly not at four in the morning. Want some cocoa?"

Lee smiled with both sides of his mouth. "Sure. I'll help boil the water."

"My hero," she said, standing. "He watches kids and boils water. What can you possibly do next?"

"Hey, watch me at about seven when it gets light," he said. "I make a really mean stack of pancakes."

Thirteen

When Lee woke in the morning, it was with a feeling of surprise. The sun was out already, streaming in the front room windows. He looked at his watch. 7:00 A.M. Cassie was already awake, smiling at him from where she was propped up on the couch. Even rumpled by a night of troubled sleep, she made a pretty picture.

"Some watchman I turned out to be," Lee said ruefully.

"Don't worry about it. I think we all slept the last few hours," Cassie said with a smile. Beside him, Lee could hear Zach stirring.

"Hey there," his mother said. "How are you doing this morning?"

The boy sat up. "It doesn't itch as bad anymore," he said.

"Good. Want to take the tape off for me while I make up a new bandage?"

Zach slipped out of his sleeping bag. "Okay. Let me go look at it in the mirror first. I want to see what I look like."

He headed down the hall and Cassie sat up and stretched. "That's a good sign. It's the first time he's shown any interest in the whole process."

"We might make it yet," Lee said, trying not to sound as shaky as he felt. Cassie rose from the couch and came over where he still sat in his sleeping bag.

She reached out and rumpled his hair. "You did fine," she told him with a smile. Lee felt his throat constrict as her innocent gesture turned into something much more powerful for both of them. "No one could have done better," she said.

"Wow. That's some compliment. Are you just buttering me up so I'll make those pancakes?" he teased. Standing, he stretched out the kinks in all those muscles cramped by a night on the floor.

"No, but I won't turn you down either," Cassie said. "Want to make coffee, too? I feel like I need my own personal pot this morning."

"The feeling is mutual. Point me to the right stuff in the kitchen, and I'll make flapjacks while you play Florence Nightingale," Lee said.

Cassie pointed him in the direction of the supplies in the pantry, and Lee put on a pot of coffee then began stirring the pancake batter. While he worked, Cassie got out sterile tape and gauze to make another bandage. Zach came into the room, holding the bandage he had already removed. "So, what do you think?" Cassie asked him.

"Can't really see much," he complained. "It just looks like I slept on my blanket and got wrinkles. Do they make that bandage stuff in other colors than white? Orange would be cool."

Cassie shook her head. "Sorry, Zach. It's white or nothing. Now let's get this lovely yellow goo put in and get the new bandage on."

Zach plopped into a kitchen chair. "Okay. Let's do it and get it over with." Lee stirred pancake batter and watched the two of them as Cassie applied the ointment and put on a fresh bandage.

So this is what it was like, having kids. Lee wasn't sure if he'd ever been so scared in his entire life as he had been the night before driving to the emergency room. Even when he was shot, he hadn't been as frightened as he was with Zach. He felt so helpless. Praying took on a new quality when it was for a child, one you cared about. A new thought struck Lee, and he had to keep his hands from shaking as he stirred the batter. What would it be like when they started to drive? Yes, this was definitely parent-phobia, he thought to himself. He had it bad. Even for a tough-guy cop.

Cassie was smoothing on the last of the bandage tape and Lee was looking for the griddle when the phone rang. "Are you up to your elbows in pancake batter, or can you answer that?" she asked him.

"I can get it," he told her, closing the cabinet door in his unsuccessful search. "Neel residence," he said into the receiver.

There was a stunned silence on the other end, then an older woman spoke. "May I speak to Cassie?"

"Just a moment," he said, motioning to Cassie and holding out the phone.

"Probably the emergency room doing a follow-up," Cassie said softly. "Who else would call this early on Sunday?" She set down the roll of tape and crossed the room to the telephone. "Hello?"

The voice she heard wasn't that of an emergency room nurse. In fact, if Cassie had chosen the person she least wanted to hear from at just this moment, it would have been the woman at the other end of the line: Dierdre.

"Cassie!" Dierdre rasped, sounding distraught. "Who was that man? I haven't been this shocked in years."

Cassie's mind reeled, wondering how she should explain. Taking a deep breath, she mentally collected herself. There was no explanation but the truth, whether Dierdre liked it or not. "That was Lee Winter."

"Did you have a man stay the night? In front of those children?" Dierdre asked, her voice rising in anger. "Why, I should come up there right now and…"

Cassie cut in quickly. "Lee stayed the night, but not the way you think. He's been here all night helping me with Zach. He had a little accident, and when we got home from the emergency room, Lee stayed to help out so we could all get some sleep."

There was a short silence on the phone. "Oh. Well, what kind of accident?" Dierdre's tone was still demanding.

"He scratched his cornea," Cassie told her, not wanting to get into all the details on the telephone with Dierdre. "But the doctor assured us he's going to be fine. Would you like to talk to him?"

"I believe so," Dierdre said.

"Grandma Neel," Cassie told Zach, who sat in the chair listening to her half of the conversation.

"Hi, Grandma," Zach said into the phone. "Yeah, but not bad. Today it only itches. I'm wearing this gross patch thing, but not for long, I hope."

He listened for a while, Cassie wondering what Dierdre was asking him. "No, I don't have one. And yes, I'd like one. Red and black, of course. Like the Bulls, Grandma."

Cassie knew right away that Dierdre was asking about some kind of sports paraphernalia or clothing. She could have told Dierdre herself what colors Zach would like, now that basketball season was in full swing. But it wouldn't mean anything to Dierdre, who didn't follow sports of any kind. "I don't know that part, Grandma. You'll have to ask my mom," Cassie heard Zach say. In a moment the phone was back in her hand.

"Okay, what part am I supposed to interpret," she said good-naturedly, hoping all this would deflect Dierdre from being disturbed about Lee.

"One of the department stores has the cutest jogging suits on sale," Dierdre said. "I wanted to get one for Zachary for Christmas, but I had no idea what size or color."

"I heard him help you out on color. And size would be a boy's ten if it looks plenty roomy. A ten-twelve pants if they come sized that way. You should see the legs on this kid," Cassie said lightly. "He's turning into a sprinter on me."

"I'm sure," Dierdre said in a clipped tone. Cassie could tell she wanted to go back to asking more questions about Lee but couldn't think of a polite way to do so.

"Anything else, Dierdre?" Cassie asked, hoping there wasn't.

"Not really. I'm still looking for something comparable for Sarah. Perhaps a charm bracelet. She could start collecting little gold charms," she said.

"That might be a good idea," Cassie said, while silently thinking she wished she could collect blue jeans with no holes in the knees instead. But Dierdre would never agree to anything that mundane as a Christmas gift. Nor would she be happy knowing that Sarah wore jeans to school nearly every day, instead of the darling jumpers they shopped for when they were together in Kansas City.

"Well, then, I won't keep you. You're probably busy saying good-bye to your, uh, guest," Dierdre said. And then hung up before Cassie could say another word.

"My mother-in-law. Brad's mother…" she explained to Lee, wondering how one referred to one's former mother-in-law to one's current gentleman caller. "Grandma Neel," she finally settled.

"I gathered," Lee said, flipping a pancake. "I've got a plate of these nearly ready. Want to go first?"

"Let's give Zach the honor," Cassie said, heading him toward the table. "He looks hungry."

"I'm starved," Zach said.

"Good. I'll get out the butter and syrup and the orange juice. And I'll have the second plate," Cassie said. By then, she thought, the butterflies in her stomach from talking to Dierdre might have settled down enough for her to eat.

Once the pancakes were done, Lee got ready to leave for home to go let Skippy out and to shower and change for church. Cassie was surprised when both kids said they wanted him to come by and pick them up for church and Sunday school.

"You think you're up to it?" she asked Zach, stroking those blond curls framing the bandage.

"Sure. It will keep my mind off the itchies," Zach said. "Besides, I've got to get used to people looking at me a little funny. I'm going to be wearing this for a couple days, and I don't really want to miss school, even though I said so last night."

"Okay," Cassie said. "I'll go shower and put on something more suitable than these lovely sweats."

Lee leaned over and gave her a quick kiss on the forehead. "Great. I'll be back in about an hour, okay?"

"Fine." Her skin tingled where his lips brushed. Cassie followed him to the door. "Lee? Thank you so much for last night. It meant a lot to me."

"It was the least I could do," he said, and turned toward the Jeep in the driveway. "Let's hope your neighbors are more tolerant than Grandma Neel. Otherwise, you're going to be the talk of the town with this vehicle here all night."

"I never thought of that," Cassie admitted. "I was so busy worrying about Zach it didn't cross my mind."

"That's my girl," Lee said. He went around the Jeep and got in, waving as he started the engine and drove off. Cassie went back inside to get ready for church so that she would present a lovelier picture when he came back.

In slightly less than an hour, all three of them were sitting in the living room, which had been cleared of sleeping bags, waiting for Lee. When she heard the Jeep in the drive again, Cassie got everybody out the door so he wouldn't have to park and come in.

"You look great," she told him, meaning every word, when she slid into the seat beside him. His navy blazer fit him perfectly, and the gray flannel slacks with it still held a sharp crease. "Almost as good as you do in uniform."

"Think so? I'm glad you noticed," Lee said. Cassie was tempted to tell him just how much she noticed. How the blue of his eyes was a shade just between the navy blazer and the pale oxford cloth shirt he wore. How the tiny bit of curl to the dark hair at the nape of his neck, fresh from a shower, was so tempting she could hardly keep her hands from him. Instead she just smiled. "And you look wonderful."

"Thank you." It was the last of her three "good" outfits he hadn't seen. The dark green corduroy jumper felt velvet smooth, and she'd actually had time to quickly iron the crisp white blouse that went with it. She felt so proud to be seen with Lee in public, and she wanted him to feel the same way about her.

At least, she thought, she wanted to look presentable if they ran into Miss Dorothy. And some second sense told her that today just might be the day.

It only took about ten minutes into the Sunday school hour for them to do just that. Cassie had gotten a welcome cup of coffee and settled down in the adult discussion group that Lee usually went to when she noticed an older African-American lady with a demeanor she could only describe as regal. She was of medium height, with a halo of short silver hair around a high-cheekboned face. She wore her simple shirtwaist dress in

135

jewel tones of magenta and royal blue as if it were a designer original, and it fit her just as well. She sat down in a chair on the other end of her row.

There were two empty seats on that end of the row, just in from the woman, and Cassie got up. She walked around the chairs, where people were still settling in before class. "Excuse me. Would you be Miss Dorothy?" Cassie asked, feeling a little foolish. What if it wasn't her?

"Yes, I'm Dorothy Adams," the older lady said. "I don't believe I've had the pleasure of meeting you, but something tells me you must be Cassie."

Cassie nodded as she felt a flush spread from the collar of her blouse as Miss Dorothy's warm brown eyes regarded her. She hoped she would be found suitable to stay in Lee's company. "Why don't you sit down next to me here and we can talk until class starts or Lee gets here," Miss Dorothy said. "Once he gets here we can't talk about him, I guess. We don't want him getting a big head, now do we?"

Cassie laughed. "He can have any size head he wants this morning. After what I put him through with my son last night, he's allowed."

"This sounds interesting," Miss Dorothy said, patting her knee. "Maybe you all can join me for a hamburger after church and tell me all about it."

"I can't think of anything I'd like better," Cassie said, meaning every word.

"Better than what?" Lee asked, coming in to sit next to her.

"Better than going out to lunch with me after church," Miss Dorothy told him. "So you better be on your best behavior. Or I'll tell her everything about you that I know and see if she still comes back with you next week."

Lee flashed her a look of mock horror. "You wouldn't do that to me, would you, Dorothy?"

"Maybe not," she admitted. "Not if you bring those sweet children with you. I hear you have two of the most wonderful children on the planet."

Cassie smiled, trying not to roll her eyes. "It's nice to hear them described that way. If we're lucky, they'll act that way at lunch."

"And if they don't, I can understand that, too," Dorothy said. "I raised four and have the grandchildren to prove it. They're not all angels all the time."

"Good. Because I expect Zachary may have used up all his angelic behavior already this morning," Cassie whispered as Bible class started. "You'll still like him, though. He's the only person I know that has a smile sweeter than Lee's."

"This I have to see," Miss Dorothy whispered back. "I can hardly wait for lunch."

Fourteen

Zach and Sarah both came out of Sunday school with Advent calendars made lovingly by hand. Zach's class had crafted theirs with flaps, which he was very proud of finishing, given his limited eye-hand coordination at the moment. They were polite when introduced to Miss Dorothy and glad to hear they were going out to lunch at one of their favorite fast food places.

Everybody piled into church in a fashion Cassie considered less dignified than it needed to be, but no one else seemed to mind. Dorothy seemed unruffled by the kids' behavior, and Cassie had to admit that she was a great influence on Zach, pointing out the right places in the hymnal without seeming to shush him the way Cassie tended to herself. There was a children's talk, about Advent again, and what that special kind of waiting could mean. Cassie was surprised when Zach not only went up to be part of the talk, but volunteered quite freely that he was waiting, with great enthusiasm, to get this bandage off his eye. And yes, he volunteered, the pastor and anybody else who wanted to could pray for him asking for quick healing if they liked.

"He seems right at home here," Dorothy whispered, leaning over to Cassie.

Cassie stifled a giggle. "If he gets anymore at home, I'm going to start worrying about him taking over for the pastor," she whispered back. "Zach doesn't often meet a stranger."

"I like that in a boy," Dorothy said. "You have to watch them a little closer, I know, especially today, but he is fun to have around, isn't he?"

"That he is," Cassie said, watching Zach as the pastor sent him, and the rest of the kids, back to their seats. "Life with Zach is never boring."

She could say the same for life with Lee, at least so far. Perhaps that was the reason that he and Zachary got along so well. They did have a lot in common. Squirming into the pew, Zach plopped himself down next to Lee, who ruffled his hair and said something to him, making him grin. All too much in common at times, she thought. Letting them sit together at lunch might be a bad idea.

As it turned out, Lee and Zach were separated at lunch by Miss Dorothy, who sat in the middle of the group and kept things lively. Cassie was so glad she was getting to know her. The older lady brought out a side of Lee that up until now she hadn't seen. He was fun to be with all the time, but around Miss Dorothy, he had a grin that nearly matched Zach's. And the older lady spoiled him silly, Cassie thought. She clucked over him, making sure he got milk with his meal, not soda, and worried that he wasn't eating as he should. Lee, of course, reassured her that he was getting plenty of good nutrition. But Cassie could see he liked being worried over a little.

Miss Dorothy also wanted to hear about Skippy, how he was doing now without the cast, and what, if any, tricks he'd learned in the last week. She was tickled to hear about his Thanksgiving bow and wanted Lee to take a picture the next time he dressed him up special. "Just don't get him any of those awful antlers for Christmas. Promise me."

Lee rolled his eyes. "Don't worry. Any dog with that much beagle in him would have those things off, and destroyed, in thirty seconds flat. I wouldn't even try. I'm just surprised he took so well to the bow."

"That's because we all told him how nice he looked," Cassie said.

"And because Mom gave him treats," Sarah said, laughing. "He likes Mom because she feeds him all the time when he's at our house."

"He likes your mother because Lee likes her," Dorothy said, a twinkle in her eye. "Dogs can tell who's important."

"This is true," Lee agreed. And then he winked at Cassie over the crowd at the booth, sending a little shiver of delight through her.

"I wish you could come with me," Lee said several weeks later as Cassie drove him to the airport.

"I know. But I'm not ready to meet your folks yet, I don't think." The holiday season had gone smoothly once Zach got his bandage off. They'd all done several things together, including going out to a tree farm in the next county and cutting down a beautiful Christmas tree that now resided in Cassie's living room. She'd known from the start that Lee was going home for Christmas, but it was still hard to say good-bye.

"They're ready to meet you," Lee said. "My mother says this is the most I've talked about anybody since my instructors at the academy. She can hardly wait to meet you."

"Well, maybe soon," Cassie said. "You said they come up to visit you some, don't they?"

"Some. They won't come much until spring," Lee said. "And

I know you don't want to uproot the kids at Christmas anyhow."

"True. Not when I have to turn loose of them already the day after," Cassie said.

"You're used to that, though, right? And I imagine that if you wanted, you could have Christmas with Dierdre, one place or another."

Cassie shook her head. "I cannot imagine Dierdre and I celebrating Christmas under the same roof. I'd feel about two feet tall by the time we unwrapped the second gift."

"That bad, huh?" Lee said with a wince.

"That bad. Think of everything you've told me about your warm family Christmases and reverse it. The one time we did have Christmas with her when the children were tiny, I thought she was going to be a basket case. The final straw was when she threw an absolute fit over the fact that none of our gifts had bows on them. I had a toddler and an infant. I was happy that the children were dressed and presentable and nobody spit up on Grandma's rug. But she was convinced that we didn't care about her because none of the gifts had bows."

Lee made a noise in the back of his throat. "Maybe she's changed."

"Maybe. But you can bet that I make sure anything I send her with the kids will have lovely, color-coordinated wrapping paper and matching ribbons. And of course, the receipt tucked unobtrusively in with the gift card because no matter what it is, she'll want to return it. But it will be nicely wrapped."

"Ah, Cassie," Lee said gently. "It's Christmas. A time of love and joy. And forgiveness. Isn't there any of that in your heart for Dierdre?"

He was right, and Cassie let out a small sigh, feeling guilty. "She makes it tough. Very tough." Lately she had felt the smallest urgings—which she suspected were from God—to try to see

Dierdre in a different light this Christmas. But her memories were too often too vivid, too hurtful.

"One thing that isn't tough," she said, purposely lightening her tone, "is celebrating Christmas with you, even though we'll be in two different states. After all, you will be calling to wish Skippy happy holidays, won't you?"

Lee's snort said it all. "You expect me to talk to the dog on the phone? I don't think so. I'll call you. I'll call the kids. But if you put the dog on the phone, I'm outta there."

"Suit yourself," Cassie said, unable to resist teasing him a little. "But think of the poor little guy, his little head on little crossed paws, wondering why Daddy hasn't called him on Christmas Day."

"Yeah. Right. That little head on those little crossed paws, sleeping under the Christmas tree because Aunt Cassie fed him half the turkey again. He'll never know I'm gone."

"You're sure you don't want me to pick you up?" she asked him minutes later as she pulled the car to the curb at Lambert Airport. Around them whirled a cacophony of blaring horns, police whistles, and engine noise from the nearly gridlocked airport traffic.

"Positive. George said it would be no problem. He's bringing back some relatives to the airport that day anyway," Lee said, giving her a quick kiss on the cheek before opening the car door.

Cassie stepped out to help him retrieve the suitcases from the trunk. "I'm going to miss you," she told him.

He gave her a dazzling smile. "Could it be that the independent Cassie Neel might be softening?" Lee put one hand on his chest in mock surprise. "Nah, not likely. But thanks for saying it, Cass. I need to hear that once in a while." His eyes met hers, his expression serious. "I'm going to miss you, Cass," he said, his voice husky. "Really miss you." He gave her a quick hug as

143

someone honked impatiently behind them.

He grabbed his bags and Cassie closed the trunk, waving as he strode through the glass doors into the airport. She again inched the car into the line of traffic and hummed along with the Christmas music on the radio as she drove away. Perhaps there was hope for her yet in this relationship. At least she felt she was making progress.

December twenty-sixth—she wasn't sure how far that progress had taken her. It felt like the same old post-Christmas blues she usually had. Another day after Christmas, and her house was a wreck. The children's gifts, those they weren't taking with them, were strewn around the living room. Their clothes, those that weren't in the two suitcases in the trunk of the car, were spewing out of drawers and hanging out of their closets in last minute packing abandon.

And of course, the children themselves had started poking each other in the back seat before they'd even gotten to Wentzville. "We've got sixty-five more miles to go," she told them, sliding a tape into the car tape player. "Ease up a little. You don't want Grandma to see this kind of behavior, do you?"

Of course they didn't. Cassie didn't yell at them too loudly because if they had to squabble with each other, better to get it out of their systems now. They seemed to know what their grandmother would and wouldn't put up with and kept relatively good behavior for the time they were with her. Of course that meant that on either end of the visit, Cassie got a day or so of awful behavior to compensate. But given the choice of her getting the awful behavior or having it reported by Dierdre, she'd take this.

"Now remember your manners while you're in Kansas City," she told them. "Zach, don't play ball in the house. And Sarah, don't go changing Grandma's radio stations to anything loud and awful."

"I won't, Mom," Sarah promised. "It's so hard to even find the radio that it isn't worth the effort. Do you know she has her radio in this weird thing called a console along with the stereo? And it still plays *vinyl records?* I asked her one time why she didn't have CDs, and she said something about them being at the bank." Sarah shook her head and Cassie watched her in the rearview mirror, wondering how to explain the generation gap in technology to her daughter. Or if it was even worth the effort.

"Well, don't play with the radio without asking, anyway," she finally said. "And help with the dishes, and remember to make your beds in the morning when you get out of them."

"We will, Mom. We don't forget everything just because we're at Grandma's," Zach said. "I hope it snows. Maybe we can use Dad's old sled if it does. The one with the red metal runners."

"I hope so, too," Cassie told him. "As long as it doesn't snow New Years' Eve, so I can pick you up on time. I want you back, guys."

"We know, Mom," Sarah said. She sounded glad to be wanted. "Lee will be back by then, won't he?"

"He should be back later today," she told them. "Maybe by the time I get back from Columbia."

"Skippy will be glad. I think he misses him. He sure liked listening to him on the phone Christmas Day, didn't he? I miss him, too," Zach admitted.

"I think we all do," Cassie said. She was surprised at how much she missed Lee. She normally didn't see him every day, anyway, but this separation had caused her to think about him more than ever before. She didn't like to consider that too soon, following the fifth grade DARE graduation in a few short weeks, she'd see him even less.

He was becoming a part of the fabric of her daily life. Now that she hadn't seen him for four days, and only talked to him once in that period of time, she missed him. Missed his smile on greeting, his deep voice crowding into her thoughts, the touch of his hand.

"Mom? Will you make Zach *stop* making that face?" Sarah said from the back seat. Now there was something she wouldn't miss, Cassie told herself. Not for several days.

Sixty-one miles to Columbia. Even at seventy miles per hour, it was going to be a long trip.

Fifteen

The trip home from Columbia seemed to take half the time of the trip there. Having the car to herself, on the highway, for over an hour, was so peaceful. Cassie always used that little jaunt for good thinking time. Today her thoughts again turned to Lee.

She needed him in her life. As hard as that was to admit, it was true. But she wasn't sure on what terms she needed him.

She'd been alone for so long, and it felt natural now. It wasn't always easy, but it was what she knew. She was learning to trust again, at least trust in God. But trusting a man was more difficult. When she found herself doing it too readily, some sneaky little part of her brain always brought up Bradley.

Of course part of trusting Bradley had been easy. He *looked* and acted so trustworthy. There was something about his personality as the slightly tweedy, but still young, college professor that invited her trust. And he did nothing to discourage that until after they were married.

After they were married he slipped a little, bit by bit. What she'd taken for deep thoughtfulness became self-centered behavior. His concern wound itself around her, changing from

147

solicitation to cloying behavior, then detachment once the children were born and required her attention.

The changes were gradual. It almost surprised her one morning to realize that, though she had a fussy preschooler and a demanding newborn, the man she married was nowhere to be found. He'd slowly changed into someone she didn't know and hardly ever saw. It was extremely difficult to convince herself that Lee wouldn't do the same thing.

He was so different, at least now. Surely someone as trustworthy and honorable as he'd shown himself to be wouldn't disintegrate into the kind of person Bradley had become. But still, the only way she could find that out was to marry him and put herself at his mercy.

And Cassie had to admit, even after her hour's thoughtful drive, she still had no clear answer about whether she was ready to do that.

When she got home, the dog was deliriously happy to see her. "How was your nap?" Cassie asked him as he bounded out of Zach's room where he'd been shut up while he was home alone. She could tell he'd spent most of his time sleeping on the bed, judging from the round indentation on the comforter. "You ready to go outside for a while? Huh? Wanna go for a walk?" The magic word made him even more frantically glad than he'd been before. She clipped on his leash and took him out for a couple blocks in the crisp winter air, glad for a chance to stretch after the drive.

When they got back to the house, she gave Skippy a drink and made herself a pot of coffee. While it brewed she turned to the answering machine; its light was flashing that she had a waiting message. It was from Lee. "I'm home," he said on the tape, causing the dog to bark at the sound of his voice. "How about if I come over about five and get Skippy? We can take him back to my place and compare holidays. I can hardly wait

148

to see you. I really missed you, Cass."

She poured herself a cup of coffee and called him back. "Five is great. That will give me enough time to take a little nap and finish spoiling the dog."

"What, you mean four days didn't give you enough time to do that?" Lee asked. His teasing tone made her smile, a thrill running through her at the thought of seeing him. "What does he weigh now, anyhow?"

"The same as when you brought him over here. And wait until you see what Zach taught him," Cassie said, wondering if Lee would appreciate having a beagle who could give high fives. Maybe not, but he had one now, she reflected. "See you soon."

At five Cassie was refreshed and ready to see Lee. When the doorbell rang, she almost beat Skippy to the door. If Lee was surprised by the enthusiastic welcome he got, he didn't show it. It felt so good to be in his arms. He brought the cold air of the outside in with him, making it even more welcome to stay there in his embrace a moment and enjoy the closeness of him.

Their kiss overpowered her senses. There was the feel of his lips on hers, warm and masculine and sweet. And he smelled of aftershave and winter cold, crisp and inviting. The twill surface of his jacket was cold to the touch, and the flannel shirt he wore underneath smooth and warm. Before Cassie could take anymore in, he was pulling away slightly.

"Cassie, have you guessed that I love you?" he asked, his voice husky, as he looked into her eyes.

Her heart pounded, and she swallowed hard. But she couldn't answer, at least not yet. She put her hand up slightly, and a moment ticked by. Lee's expression changed as Skippy yipped and danced at their feet.

"I know, I know, you missed me too," he said as he patted the dog on the head. "Let Cassie get her coat on, and we'll go for a ride in the car and you can really go nuts."

He turned back to Cassie. "What do you say we get something carry out, anything other than pizza, and just plan on eating at my place?"

"Sounds great," Cassie said. "How about Chinese, with lots of strange vegetables the kids would hate? I want to live like a grown-up, at least for a day or two."

"Let's do it," Lee said. "Should we get the leash?"

The dog bounded up in the air, barking. "Wait," Cassie said. "Let's show your daddy your new trick. Come here, Skippy. Sit. Now give me five." On cue the little dog came over, sat obediently, and raised one paw in the air, not putting it down until he tapped Cassie's palm with it.

"Is that what Zach taught him?" Lee asked with a laugh. "That's great."

"He worked hard on it. He'll be glad you like it."

"I'll have to be sure to tell him first thing when I see him," Lee said. "Now how about we hit the town?"

Cassie wondered, on the way over, what Lee's condo would look like. She hadn't been there before, and he'd played it down when he described it, calling it "your typical bachelor place." She knew there couldn't be much to it, but then a man as busy as Lee, and single, didn't need much space.

The complex was nice, and only about a mile from the Chinese restaurant where they'd stopped and ordered dinner to go. So things were still piping hot in their cartons when they got to Lee's kitchen. It wasn't as big as Cassie's or as well equipped. But it did have a nice breakfast bar between the kitchen and the great room, where Lee had already set two places for dinner.

"Planning ahead, were we?" Cassie said, looking at the plates and cloth napkins.

"Hope springs eternal," Lee said. "Do you use chopsticks, or should I get out forks?"

"Both," Cassie said. "I've never tried chopsticks, but I'm willing to give it a go. However, I also don't want to starve to death, so I'd better have a fork handy."

"The ever practical Cassie," Lee said, setting out the cartons of Chinese food. "While I do this, tell me about your Christmas. Then while we eat, I'll tell you about mine."

"Good choice. You'll probably have more to tell me than I will to tell you," Cassie said. "You've heard my best stories already on the phone Christmas Day. And I suspect from the happy crowd noises behind you, I haven't heard the half of your stories."

"Crowd noises?" Lee protested. "Those were not crowd noises. Just my mom and dad, my sister and her husband, and their two kids. The other relatives hadn't even gotten there yet."

"Okay, I stand corrected," Cassie said. "But it sure sounded lively. Remember, I'm used to holidays for three."

"Well, it did get pretty spirited," Lee said. "Especially when they all started giving me a hard time about not bringing you and the kids. Or even a picture. I didn't even have pictures of Skippy. I was not in my aunts' good graces all afternoon, let me tell you."

He got serious then, as he slid into his seat next to Cassie on one of the stools at the breakfast bar. "They really do want to meet you soon. I promised my folks that we would find a way to get together."

Cassie swallowed hard and looked at the cartons of food. It felt easier to do that than to look at Lee's face. "Wow. Going home to meet the folks. This sounds serious, Lee."

"I guess it is," he said. "I haven't brought anybody home to meet them. Not like this. But Cassie, I'm ready to do it now. Are you?"

She had to look at him then. His voice was so serious. "I don't know. I think so, Lee. But I have my doubts."

"About what? What have I given you doubts about?"

"Not you, exactly. It's me. And the kids."

"Your kids like me, Cass. Try to tell me they don't."

"I know they like you. I like you." She smiled gently. "Let me rephrase that, I think I love you."

"Think?" Lee's brow furrowed. "Why does it seem you're about to add a 'but' to that?"

She drew in a deep breath. "I wonder if you've thought this through, Lee. I've got two kids and a lot of baggage here. And I'm not sure I'm ready."

"You don't have to be ready right this minute, Cass," Lee said, meeting her gaze. She tried to read his expression. Though intense, it was calm. It seemed he was settling something in his mind. It was almost as if he was withdrawing from her…or maybe releasing her. "You want to eat before the food gets cold?" he asked suddenly.

Cassie nodded, still studying his face.

He reached for the beef and broccoli, handing her the carton. "How about an egg roll?"

She set down her chopsticks next to her full plate. "I don't understand. I tell you that I need time, and you seem to be more interested in dinner than talking about what really matters. It's not like you."

Lee put down his chopsticks as well, this time meeting her gaze with a half smile. "I love you, Cassie. But you have some things to work through on your own. And they're between you and the Lord. No matter how much I try, I can't do that for you. All I can do is leave it all in his hands."

"So for now it's better to pretend that it doesn't matter?" Cassie asked, feeling brittle and a little hurt.

Lee's blue eyes held so much emotion when he looked at her and took her hands in both of his. "Is that what it feels like to you? Trust me. That isn't what I'm trying to do. You've got to understand, Cass. I've given this all to God. What he's going to do with it, I can't tell." He squeezed her hands in his earnestness. "I love you, Cassie, but I can't wear my heart on my sleeve. I've had coffee with friends on the force at ten at night, then watched them die before midnight. If we're going to be together, you have to get used to that part of me."

He was so open and honest. It was just one more reinforcement for her that he wasn't Brad. Would never be Brad, but remain Lee, plain spoken, solid and up-front. She looked down at his hands holding hers. His fingers were long and beautifully tapered, and there was a glint of gold in the fine sprinkling of hair.

"So you do worry that we might not stay together? And most of that worry comes from where I am with God?"

Lee nodded. "It does."

"But you're not going to push me just so our relationship can be—" she struggled for the word "—complete."

"I can't, Cass. You have to do this by yourself."

"Okay. I understand," she said, looking back up at his earnest face. "As for what I was talking about earlier, let me ask you again. One more time, just so I get it right. I'm thirty-three years old. A widow with two kids, one of whom is closing in fast on being a teenager. And none of that bothers you?"

"None of it," Lee said. "The teenager stuff maybe a little. But I'll be just as nervous when Zach hits the same age. And any other kids we might have."

Cassie felt her head begin to spin. "Other kids?"

His brow furrowed again. "Is this some of what you're trying to tell me? That you think you're too old to have any more? Or that you can't, maybe?"

"No. Not at all," she said, the words tumbling out. "It's just that...I hadn't given it much thought. I love kids. I've just never known a man before who really wanted them. Bradley wasn't exactly tickled pink when Sarah came along."

Lee shook his head. "I'm sorry to hear that. I love you so much, I can't imagine not loving your kids. The blessing of children is one of the reasons I want to get married. Sarah and Zach will be as much a blessing to me as anybody else who comes along later."

Cassie felt as if she had been given a gift beyond price. "You really mean that," she said, softly.

"I really mean that. If it will help you get used to the idea of my sticking around for good, I'll tell you once or twice a day for a few weeks."

"Once every couple days will be enough," Cassie said, leaning over and going forehead to forehead with the incredible man in front of her. When she leaned her lips into his, it was the first kiss she had offered him, instead of him taking one from her. And it was the most wonderful kiss she could ever remember.

❧

"Keep the pieces away from the edges," Cassie warned Lee, as she turned over bright bits of a jigsaw puzzle. "The last thing I want that dog to eat is part of this puzzle."

"Yeah," Lee said, moving around the various pieces with his long, slender fingers. "It's hard to finish a field of flowers when somebody eats the daffodils."

"It wouldn't be any good for his digestion, either," Cassie warned him. "Why don't I get him a rawhide chewie, just to distract him?"

154

"He knows the word," Lee told her. "Did you see how his ears perked up?"

"Rawhide," Cassie said, just to test him. Skippy's tail thumped on the carpet, and he yipped. "You're right. Well, follow me to the kitchen and we'll get one." The dog trotted after her, looking pleased with himself.

"Should I put a bag of popcorn in the microwave while I'm in here?" Cassie called out to Lee.

"Sure. Sounds good," he called back. She rummaged in the pantry, wondering where the last bag of popcorn had gotten to. Without the kids to cook for she would have been forced to admit that what meals she hadn't eaten with Lee had been an odd combination of things like cold cereal and popcorn out of the microwave bag. Somehow it had been fun not to cook, not to worry about serving nutritious balanced meals at regular times just for a couple days. Tonight, with company, she would be formal and get out a bowl for the popcorn.

She was looking in the cabinets, trying to decide which one of her bowls would hold the most popcorn when the telephone rang. "Hello," she said, one hand still in the cabinet.

"Cassie? Good. I was beginning to think I wouldn't reach you today," Dierdre said smoothly. So the three hang ups on the answering machine earlier had been her.

"Well, I'm here now," Cassie said, unwilling to rise to the bait. "How are the kids?"

"Good." Dierdre's answer was short, even for her. At least she usually volunteered more than this.

"Have they given you any trouble?" Cassie asked, wondering if that was the reason for the call.

"Not at all. They'd never give me a moment's trouble," Dierdre said. Again, her voice sounded too smooth.

Cassie began to feel uneasy. There was something about Dierdre's tone that disturbed her. "That's good to hear. I know they're active. Zach was really hoping it would snow so that they could use Bradley's sled," she told her. "Without any snow, I'm sure they've kept you busy. You'll probably be ready to meet me Monday in Columbia so you can get some rest."

"That's why I was calling," Dierdre said. "We won't be coming Monday."

"If you need to make it tomorrow instead, I understand," Cassie said, suddenly eager to have her children back. "It wouldn't bother me. Lee's off tomorrow, and he could drive up with me. It would give you a chance to meet."

"No, you don't understand," Dierdre broke in. "I don't want to give them back earlier, Cassandra. I don't want to give them back at all."

She couldn't be hearing this right. "What do you mean, Dierdre?"

"Exactly what I said. I've been talking to them for days. And frankly, I don't see why I should give them back. I have real doubts about your fitness as a parent. I intend to see my lawyer Monday. About getting custody."

The heavy ironstone bowl that Cassie had finally found thudded on the countertop, and she sat on the cold kitchen floor. Puzzled, Skippy came over and climbed in her lap. She pushed him away with rapidly numbing fingers. "You can't be serious."

"Oh, I'm terribly serious. The stories these children have told me in the last few days have really upset me," Dierdre said, her tone now cold and angry. "How you leave them alone at all hours, risking their lives while you go off with that man. How you wrecked your car and let Zachary injure himself, severely. I may be nearly sixty, Cassandra, but I'm willing to take on raising children again to keep them from something like that."

"You've got things all mixed up, Dierdre," Cassie sputtered. "That just isn't the way things happened."

"I expected you to deny it," Dierdre said.

Cassie drew in a deep breath. "Whether you believe me or not, there is no way I'd let you even consider keeping my children. Do they know about your plan?"

Her question was met by silence.

"Let me talk to them!" Cassie demanded. "Now!"

"I'm sure that wouldn't be for the best," Dierdre said, her voice sounding far away in Cassie's ear. "In fact, I think I've said all I need to." And then there was a click, followed by a dial tone.

Cassie dialed Dierdre's number with shaking fingers. Busy. "She took it off the hook," she said to the empty kitchen. "She took it off the hook." Leaning against the cabinet, the tears started.

"Lee," she called. "I need you. In here, right now." He was there almost before the words had left her lips, and Cassie slid to the floor, overwhelmed by grief and fear.

Sixteen

*L*ee looked over at Cassie. Pale and red eyed, she hadn't said anything for half an hour. There were so many questions he needed to ask her. So many things he wanted to get out of the way before they got anywhere near Kansas City and the confrontation he knew was coming.

As he drove, he prayed silently. And he reflected on Miss Dorothy's words about prayer. She often reminded him to be careful what he asked for, because he'd get it. "In the Lord's way, Lee. Not yours," she was always saying.

So many times over the last few months, Lee had prayed for Cassie to discover that she wanted him in her life. But this wasn't what he had in mind. He wanted Cassie to want Lee Winter, all around nice guy and husband material. Lee Winter, possible father to two wonderful kids. Not Lee Winter, cop who might have to check in with Kansas City's finest and execute court custody documents. But he hadn't been specific in his prayers. And Cassie sure wanted and needed him now.

The road signs pointed to gasoline and fast food outlets at the next exit. "I need a break, Cass. And we need to talk. How about something to eat and a stop for a little while, okay?"

"If you're hungry, that's fine," Cassie said. "I don't think I can eat."

"Try something. Maybe just a carton of milk," Lee said, trying not to sound too paternal. "You need to be at your best when we get to Dierdre's."

"I don't think I have any strength left, Lee. I don't understand how this can be happening." She paused. "And I'm still trying to convince myself that this isn't another example of God punishing me somehow."

"It isn't, Cass," he said, turning off the highway. "It's one of the few things I'm sure of in this situation. It may be a test, but it's not a punishment. That's not the way God works. He loves you, he loves Zach and Sarah, and he loves Dierdre. Let's try to keep all of that in mind."

"Seeing Dierdre in that light is hardest. I really felt that God was softening my heart toward her," Cassie said. "But now…" her voice faltered, and Lee wanted to reach over and stroke her hair, pat her shoulder, hug her, anything to bring her comfort. But he knew the only thing that was going to make her feel better was having Zach and Sarah back in her arms.

They went into the restaurant. Lee could tell the bright colors and lights were nearly overwhelming Cassie. She slipped off to wash her face and came back clear eyed and without the shaking hands he'd noticed earlier. Lee ordered himself lunch and looked at Cassie. "A carton of milk," she told the girl working the counter.

Lee carried the tray to a far booth. Cassie slid in on the other side from him and took his hands once he was settled.

"I never thought I'd be comfortable enough to ask this of you, but please say grace with me," Cassie said. "Right here, in front of who knows what kind of crowd."

Lee found himself praying softly around a lump in his throat. He ached for Cassie and for what she was going

160

through. But if this is what it took for the Father to complete the work he'd begun in her life, Lee couldn't argue. He thought of his own turning point in a hospital bed years before, a bullet high in his shoulder. He'd take a bullet any day to what Cassie was going through.

Once they were settled and Cassie was sipping her milk, Lee spoke again. "Okay, I need to know all the information you can give me before we get to Kansas City, Cass. Tell me everything that led up to today."

"Where do I start?" she said, one hand lifted, empty palm up.

"Wherever the beginning is. If I'm going to help you, I have to know everything. There's been so much hidden between us," Lee said. "Now I have to know it all."

"Nobody knows it all," Cassie said. "I don't even know it all. I'll never know what was in Bradley's mind in the months before he died. Before he nearly divorced me."

Lee felt his head snap up in surprise. "What? I thought you were a widow."

"I was. But if Brad had lived just a little longer, I wouldn't have been." And she told him a story that was as strange as anything he'd heard on the streets in his years as a police officer. Lee's lunch, long forgotten, grew cold as he listened to her story with growing surprise and anger.

"And Dierdre doesn't know any of this?" he asked, knowing that he wasn't covering the amazement in his voice.

"Not from me," Cassie said. "And no one else really knew all of it. I didn't find out about the graduate student until I met her at the cemetery later in the week. She didn't have to tell me about her relationship with Brad. I knew." She swallowed hard. "If anyone else at the college knew, they didn't volunteer the information to me, or to Brad's mother."

She straightened her shoulders and sat taller in the booth,

her brown eyes glowing with unshed tears. "I had children to raise. What good would it have done to tell them that their father was no good? That instead of the intelligent, funny, witty man I was presenting to them, they knew about the guy who wouldn't have changed a diaper if his life depended on it and was leaving me for someone else because she was younger and smarter."

"None, I guess," Lee said. "At least not yet. But his mother might have treated you differently if she'd known some of this."

"She might have. And she might have decided a few years earlier than she did that I wasn't fit to raise her precious grandchildren. After all, her son didn't think I was fit to keep."

"But he wouldn't have tried for custody, would he?"

"Bradley? Not likely. I probably would have had a running battle for child support, never mind custody," Cassie said. "In that respect, I guess I was fortunate."

"It's sure destroyed your trust in the human race. At least half of it," Lee said.

"That it has. Until you came along," Cassie said. "You've really convinced me that not every man is like Brad. That there might still be men out there who mean what they say and have the actions to back up their words."

"That's what I'm here for, Cass," he told her, reaching out for that slender cool hand. She clutched his hand like a lifeline, and Lee prayed silently that he was up to the job she had planned for him.

"Do you think she'll let us in? That she'll be there at all?" Lee asked once they were on the road again. It was his major worry, that Dierdre's call the night before was just a warning before she took off for parts unknown.

"If she's there she'll let us in. Or at least open the door and harangue us. And I can't see Dierdre leaving with the kids," she said with a deep sigh. "At least I hope she truly cares about them enough not to subject them to something like that."

"She has to realize that she doesn't have a leg to stand on," Lee said. "There's never been the slightest hint that anyone except you should have custody."

"I wonder, though, if the simple fact that he left his mother legally in charge of the children's finances might make a judge wonder about my competency." Lee reached for her hand as she went on.

"That same financial arrangement guaranteed that Dierdre would always be in the picture," Cassie said. "And you have to realize he was raised a whole different way than you or I. At least I'm making an assumption here that you weren't raised in the lap of luxury, with private schools and your own pony."

"Are you kidding? I didn't even have my own car until I was nineteen and bought one for two hundred dollars. It ran for three months," Lee said, laughing a little. "My dad told me to go back to my bicycle until I could afford a car that ran. He said it would teach me something about picking out vehicles."

"I'll bet it did," Cassie said. "Bradley wasn't taught the value of anything, I don't think. Except himself. He valued himself very highly. And his family connections, and the fact that he was a respected professor on his way to the tenure track. It really bothered him that I enjoyed staying home making Play-Doh for the kids."

"Not up to his social standards?" Lee asked.

"Exactly," Cassie said. "I should have spent more time involved with faculty wives' activities and volunteer stuff. That was all so foreign to me that I never felt like I fit in with the rest of the group."

"He had to have known that when you got married," Lee said.

"When we got married, I'm sure Bradley saw this pretty girl that he could mold into anything he liked. And he got her for a little while." Her smile was sad. "But then she grew up a little and had two children. And became a mommy that bored him out of his skull."

"You'll never bore me, Cass," Lee said, taking one hand off the wheel to squeeze hers. *Not if we have a dozen kids for you to mother,* he added silently, then wondered where that came from. Right now he was just hoping to get her kids back where they belonged. How he could handle more than that was beyond him.

"So she'll probably be there," Lee went on, going back to the problem at hand. "And she'll probably open the door. What do we do then?"

"Ask to be invited in," Cassie said. "With Dierdre one does not invite oneself. Not even in dire circumstances. With any luck, she'll be keeping things civil. She's probably hoping that I've come to discuss things. If she's feeling generous, she might even offer to let me move in with them if I could find a suitable job in the area."

Her face looked a little drawn, set in a determined fashion while she looked out to the ribbon of highway stretching in front of them. "What she doesn't know is that I don't intend to play nice. That if she asks me in, I'm not leaving that house until those kids go with me."

"That's where we're going to have to be careful," Lee warned her. "I want the same thing, but we can't terrify the kids. Or call in the reinforcements unless I have to. Do you think she's con- tacted her attorney yet?"

Cassie shook her head. "No, because of the timing. Dierdre is a pretty stubborn lady. Once she makes up her mind about something, she doesn't expect any challenges. So to her this is cut and dried. She will, eventually, call in the lawyers and get things moving. But chances are good she doesn't expect anything more out of me than my bringing the children's clothes, or maybe asking to move back here to Kansas City to be near them. She wouldn't dream that I'd actually fight her."

"Then she doesn't know you very well," Lee said.

"That's part of the problem." Cassie sounded close to tears again. "She never has known me very well. Or wanted to. For Dierdre Neel, I was just an incubator. A warm body that provided her with grandchildren to be first a wonderful addition to, and then a replacement for, her precious son. She never has considered me a human being with feelings."

"You really hate her, don't you?"

Cassie was silent for a while. "At times I've tried not to, especially lately. But now that she has my children…" she said softly before her voice faltered. "I honestly think you're right."

"What does it gain, Cass? Other than pain and suffering? It will just eat at you inside."

"You haven't met her," Cassie said, finally looking for a tissue in her purse. "There's so much to dislike. Not that she's evil or anything, really. Just extremely self-centered. I don't think Dierdre can imagine a world run a different way than she wants it run. Brad helped her achieve that, at least as far as his family was concerned, by appointing her executor of his estate. She figures that she's the one with control of the money, so she should also decide how the children are raised. And this time I stepped too far over the line in making my own wishes known."

"Well, wait till she gets a load of Cassie Neel, mama tiger," Lee said. "Just keep those claws sheathed for me as long as possible, okay? I don't have many contacts in Kansas City, and I don't want us spending any time in a lockup someplace. Deal?"

"Deal," Cassie said, still sounding a little shaky as she wiped her eyes with the tissue she'd now crumpled. "For a little while, at least. I wish we'd brought Skippy instead of leaving him with George. If he saw anybody upsetting Zach, he'd be a great addition to the troops."

Lee shook his head. "I am not teaching that sweet little dog to be a guard animal. And especially not on older ladies, no matter what they do."

"Rats," Cassie said. "He wouldn't have to bark or bite or anything. Just the possibility of him shedding on the oriental rugs would probably be enough."

"We'll find a way to solve this," Lee promised. "A way that doesn't hurt anyone. A way that honors God." And silently he hoped that the Lord would show him. Because with only twenty-nine miles to go, Lee had no idea what that way was going to be.

Seventeen

ee didn't know what he was expecting once they got to Kansas City. Something like that black-and-white, 1930s movie version of *Heidi,* maybe, with some dried-up looking woman standing like a dragon in front of Zach and Sarah. But instead of some imposing mansion, Dierdre lived in a nice, although fairly ordinary-looking, brick house in an older suburb.

It was neatly kept, with the lawns showing that either the fifty-seven-year-old woman did a lot of work or had a good gardener. What made Lee's spirits sink when they pulled up to the house was that it didn't look occupied. "I don't think there's anybody here, Cass," he said. There were certainly no children outside, and no blinds or curtains open. No lights shone through any of the windows, and the morning newspaper was still on the fieldstone front porch.

"Maybe they went out shopping or something," Cassie said, a note of panic in her voice. "She wouldn't have gone far with them. I know that much."

Lee wanted it to be true for Cassie's sake. "Then we'll wait," he said. "Unless you have a key to the house."

"Are you kidding? I'm lucky to have the address and phone number. Even when Bradley was alive I didn't have a key to this house."

"Okay. I didn't think so, but it's always worth a try," Lee said. "You want the radio on?"

"No. I do want to hold hands, though."

Cassie's hand was cold. No matter how long Lee held it, it didn't seem to warm up. They sat for half an hour or better and her hand was still cold, and the driveway remained empty.

"I guess you were right," Cassie finally said, in a voice that sounded so heartbroken that Lee ached for her. "What do we do now?"

Lee looked around. "How friendly is Dierdre with her neighbors?"

"Somewhat. Why?"

"Because across the street a gentleman just came out to do yard work. I'm tempted to go talk to him."

Cassie's hand was on the door latch immediately. "I'm going with you."

Jim Wilson appeared to be about seventy, dressed in a battered jacket and heavy twill pants. "Didn't get to trim all the dead flowers from that front bed this fall," he said as Lee and Cassie started up the walk to his white Cape Cod style house. "Had a bit of gall bladder surgery, and the missus didn't let me do anything heavy for a while. Can I help you folks?"

Lee introduced himself and Cassie. "We were looking for Dierdre and the kids," he said, trying to sound nonchalant. "We were supposed to meet them in Columbia tomorrow but thought we'd come all the way over and surprise them."

"That's a shame," Wilson said, making Lee's heart sink. "You shoulda called first. They all took off early this morning, before Dee usually leaves for church. Had a couple suitcases with them, so I bet they were going somewhere overnight. She came over and gave Maudie a key, asked her to get the mail and papers for a few days. You think she buzzed over to Columbia early? I know they've got a Holidome there. Kids sure love those indoor pools. At least my grandchildren always do."

Beside him, Lee felt Cassie stiffen. "I guess that could be," he said, reaching out and holding her hand.

"There isn't anything wrong?" Jim Wilson had a look of concern growing on his face.

"Not yet. But I'd appreciate you giving me your phone number," Lee said. "Cass and I better grab two motel rooms for the night and wait for them to come back."

"That's kind of silly, isn't it? When we have the key to across the street. Dee wouldn't mind you staying there while you wait for her, would she?" Jim asked. "She talks about those kids all the time. They're just the apple of her eye."

Cassie's grip felt even tighter in his hand now. Lee could feel her body trembling, on the edge of panic. "That would be great, Mr. Wilson," he told the older man. "We'd really appreciate it."

Mr. Wilson went in the house to get the key from his wife. "Dierdre will go ballistic if and when she gets back and finds out we've been in that house," Cassie said softly.

"Maybe so," Lee told her. "But that's the least of my concerns right now. If we get in there, maybe we can figure out where she's gone."

The furrows of worry on Cassie's face smoothed a little. "Oh. I didn't think of it that way. I guess it's a gift from God that I've got a policeman helping me look for my kids."

She said it so naturally that Lee almost laughed out loud. But Jim chose that moment to return, so he stayed silent. "I guess it is," he said softly. "Now let's get over there and get busy looking."

∿ ∿ ∿ ∿ ∿

Cassie felt strange going through Dierdre's house without her in it. She couldn't think of a time this had ever happened, even for a few moments. It was so quiet and tidy that it was hard to believe that Dierdre and her children had been living there just hours before.

There were no dirty dishes in the sink, or any other evidence in the stark blue-and-white kitchen that they'd had breakfast before they left. It was only when they got to the bedrooms in their search that Cassie could see any evidence that her children had been there for almost a week.

"They didn't take everything with them," Lee said, holding up one of Zach's T-shirts. "That's a good sign."

"Is it?" Cassie felt so numb, as if she'd been out in a snowbank too long. Everything came to her from a great distance and felt sort of muted.

"Trust me, it is. If she was going to flee with the kids for a long while, on purpose, she'd have packed everything they owned. This looks like they're planning on coming back. That or she's not very good at this. Either way, it will make them easier to find."

"I hope so," Cassie said fervently. "I can't imagine not finding them. I can't even imagine not finding them today. Oh, Lee, what am I going to do?"

The tears finally overwhelmed her, and she sat down on the narrow twin bed in Brad's old room, clutching the bed pillow. It still smelled of Zachary and she clung to it, unable to stop crying.

"Cass, we *are* going to find them," Lee said gently. "Let me look around a little more. She has to have left something that will tell us where they went." Lee put his arm around her shoulder, and Cassie leaned against him, taking comfort in his presence. But it wasn't enough, wouldn't be enough, until her children were back in her arms.

An hour later Lee looked baffled. His dark hair showed the evidence of his fingers raking through it more than once in frustration. "She had to have left something," he said.

"You don't know Dierdre. She's a very methodical person, and bright as well. I can imagine her being able to cover her tracks for quite a while."

"Let's look at the kids' things again, see what they took and what they didn't," Lee said, heading for Bradley's old bedroom again.

"That may be a little difficult," Cassie said. "We can narrow it down to a point, but I'm not sure what Dierdre bought them for Christmas. For all I know, they might each have a complete new wardrobe that she's taken with them."

Lee shook his head. "Zach and Sarah are smart kids. That would tip them off that something was up, and I can't imagine either of them going willingly if that was the case. Sarah, especially, is old enough to use a phone and get to you."

"I'm sure you're right," Cassie said. "I guess I have to believe in that, don't I?"

Lee turned to face her. "We both have to, Cass. We both have to trust that they're all in God's care and will come back here. Maybe in his time, but they'll come back."

Cassie felt her stomach clench again. "What do you mean, 'his time?' That it might be a while?"

Lee came toward her, looking cautious. "It could be. Or she could come back with them but be determined to try a custody battle. And I don't know about you, but I wouldn't want to drag the kids out of here physically if there was another way to solve things. Let's face it, the bottom line is that we want Zach and Sarah back in the way that's going to be best for them first, then best for everybody else second. Agreed?"

Cassie sighed. Lee was right. "Agreed. But I sure hope 'his time' isn't a much different timetable than mine, because I don't know how long I can stand this."

He let out a deep sigh. "I'm with you, Cass. More than a few more hours and I'm going to be a basket case. And they're not even my kids." Lee ran his fingers through his wavy hair again and looked around the room. "I don't think this is going to tell us anything else." He paused thoughtfully. "How about we go somewhere close and grab something to eat, then come back here and I'll start calling my few friends on the force in Kansas City, okay?"

Cassie looked around the room, seeing for the first time in hours that it was late in the afternoon. Lee was probably starving. For herself, she felt as if food would stick in her throat if she even tried, but she knew he would urge her to eat something to keep up her strength. "All right," she told him. "Just make sure it's very close. I want to be back here in less than an hour." *And I want my kids back even before that,* she added silently, knowing even as she said it that it wasn't going to happen.

Lee urged her to eat at the steak house they found close to Dierdre's. Cassie finally got a bowl of soup and some bread off the buffet and was surprised that it tasted good. Maybe she did need to eat after all, she conceded. To prove to Lee that she was serious about keeping up her strength, she let him fix her a sundae afterwards as well. Most of it melted into a dribbly pile in the dish, but she did eat a few bites.

It was difficult to eat, wondering what the kids were doing and where they were. She knew that Dierdre wouldn't mistreat them in any way. Wherever they were, they were probably having the time of their lives. She wondered if Dierdre had told them why they weren't at her house. Silently in the crowded restaurant she prayed that Dierdre was keeping them innocent of the changes she intended to inflict on their lives.

"I'm going to get a cup of coffee," Lee said, breaking into her thoughts. "Then let's go back to the house, and I'll make some phone calls."

Cassie nodded. Anything that might bring her children back soon was fine.

The phone calls, when Lee made them, frustrated them both more than they helped. "So let me get this straight," Cassie said, pacing in Dierdre's well-appointed living room. "If they haven't been gone more than twenty-four hours, and we have no reason to think she's taken them over state lines, the police can't do anything?"

"Not a thing. I was afraid of that, but I was hoping, since she's a noncustodial grandparent who made a threat to keep them, we could get somebody to see it our way," Lee said. "Unfortunately, nobody does."

"This is ridiculous!" Cassie fumed. "I have to wait another twelve hours or so until I can report my own kids missing?"

"That's the way it looks," Lee said. "How about if we go for a walk outside and talk about this. There's other things we need to talk about too, Cass."

Something in his expression made her agree without hesitation. She bundled up in the warm clothing she'd brought and made sure Dierdre's house key was in her pocket.

There were stars in the sky. Cassie could see them glittering overhead. It seemed ironic, somehow, that things were going on as usual when her life was so horribly wrong. Dierdre's neighborhood was quiet. Cars were parked in front of several houses, promising holiday gatherings of friends or families inside, but on the street there was little noise.

"I miss my dog," Lee said, looking up at the sky with her.

Holding his hand, even when they both wore gloves, was reassuring. "It feels strange to be going on a walk without Skippy."

"Everything about this walk feels strange," Cassie said. "No Skippy, no Zach, no Sarah. Even the stars feel a little out of place two hundred miles from where I usually see them."

"That's not all that's out of place, Cass."

The stars froze in their places, and Cassie's heart froze with them. "What do you mean?" They stopped under a streetlight, and Cassie could see from the set of Lee's face that he'd been considering what to say for quite a while.

He let go of her hand. Cassie felt so cold, and terribly alone, just from losing his touch.

"This is hard to say, Cass. I love you. I want to make a life with you. But I want all of you, free and clear."

"You have that now, Lee," she said softly.

"No, I don't think I do, Cass. Now that I know what you've been through with Dierdre…and what happened with Brad…I believe you have some unfinished business before you can come to me."

"Unfinished business?" Cassie stepped back from him. She shook her head incredulously. "We do have some unfinished business here, Lee Winter. My children are missing. That's more unfinished business than I ever wanted in a lifetime," Cassie said, her bitter words carried away by the winter breeze.

"That's true. But, Cassie, I see how you're struggling with the hurt and resentment in your heart. Sometimes, I think it might consume you." He stepped closer, and his voice softened. "I think you need to confess it, first to God, and then to Dierdre when we find her. There can't be healing, Cass, until there's forgiveness."

Cassie stood speechless. "Ask for Dierdre's forgiveness? For what? For putting up with her all these years? For begging for money to put clothing on my children's backs? For nearly going crazy while she takes them away from me?" She turned away from Lee, trying to hold back her tears of frustration and anger. "I can't do that."

Lee's tone was urgent. "Cass, your burden is too heavy to carry alone. God is waiting for you to give it to him."

Cassie whirled to face him. Her dismay washed over her in waves, the way it had the night Brad died. "I can't believe you could ask this of me! Especially tonight." The clear air rang with her words, harsh in the puff of warm breath she expelled. "It's unbearable to even think of it!"

"Oh, Cass," her name on his lips came out a sigh. "I'm not asking it. Jesus is. You're carrying a burden of resentment, anger, and hurt. It doesn't have to be that way. He died to take our burdens from us. To heal us, make us whole." He paused. "And hard as it is to think about right now, Jesus died for Dierdre, too. Can't you forgive her—even as he's forgiven you? Forgive her in his name?" He paused, then added. "Even tonight?"

She stared at Lee, her lips pressed together. Finally she spoke. "No, I can't, Lee. It's impossible."

"You're right, Cassie," he said after a moment. "It is impossible, humanly impossible."

"Then what else do you require?" she snapped, ignoring his meaning. "That I forgive Brad, too?"

Lee nodded silently. "It's not my requirement, Cassie. It's God's."

Lee was asking too much. God was asking too much. "I think you need to go," she finally managed. Cassie felt that she was holding herself still so that she wouldn't shatter. So that she wouldn't break apart in a million brittle pieces, as she awaited his response.

It wasn't long in coming. "If that's the way you feel, maybe I had better leave," Lee said. It was the last thing either of them said on the cold walk back to Dierdre's house.

Eighteen

romise me you'll think about all this, Cassie. Pray about it," Lee said softly, but with intensity. "Anything that will make you consider it, Cass."

"I'll think. And I'll pray," Cassie promised. But inside her head, the same litany was playing over and over. *This is too hard. This is too much to ask. I just can't do this.* Lee kissed her softly and left. She closed the door on the cold outside, and on Lee. And inside her head, the same phrases kept playing over and over.

She regretted Lee leaving the moment she saw the taillights of the car pull away. Not because she was now stranded at Dierdre's house. If she had to be somewhere without her kids, it was as good a place as any. But remembering the hurt on Lee's face tore her apart. And wondering where he was kept her awake most of the night as she lay on Zach's bed, surrounded by his pillows, and a few others from Sarah's daybed, still holding the scent of her shampoo. If Cassie slept, it was for a very short time.

I can't do this. What he asks is impossible. It is too hard.

The same mocking phrases were still playing the next

morning when she dragged herself to Dierdre's kitchen after her rocky night's sleep. How could Lee be so out of touch with her feelings that he would ask this of her? What place was it of his to tell her how to feel and how to run her life? She went mechanically through the steps of putting on coffee and finding her Bible.

The sky outside wasn't pearl pink with the promise of dawn. This morning it looked more like lead. Dull, iron gray clouds reflected very little of the sunlight Cassie knew was there someplace.

She poured herself a cup of coffee when it finished brewing and sat at the kitchen table, her Bible in front of her. The rosy pink cover seemed to mock her. She knew it couldn't help her closed like this. But the energy to open it, search for what she needed, just wasn't there. So she sat, sipping her cooling coffee and wondering what to do next.

She needed someone to talk to. Someone warm and real, and God felt a thousand miles away. "And the one person who would understand all this is gone because I kicked him out," she said to the empty kitchen, her words bouncing off the white walls.

Her gaze locked on the phone. She could call someone. But who? Her own mother would only fall apart, upset by everything Cassie would tell her. There were no friends from work who were close enough to hear this whole story. As she thought, a picture of warm brown eyes and a crown of silver hair formed in her mind. *Miss Dorothy.* Somehow Cassie knew she would know what to say, or at least be able to listen the right way. Punching up the numbers for Information, Cassie prayed that Dorothy was listed in the phone book.

In a few moments Dorothy had answered the telephone and was listening just as Cassie had hoped.

She was troubled that Dierdre had the children and listened

quietly while Cassie told her about Lee's thoughts of the night before. "And I just can't do it, Dorothy," she concluded.

This was difficult to admit aloud. What Lee asked sounded perfectly reasonable on the surface. This would all be over soon, Cassie told herself. She should go to Dierdre, ask her forgiveness, and get on with life. She should mentally dump all the garbage from Brad and her past that she'd been carrying. Then she could start fresh without all the suspicions and anger and hurt. But every time she pictured Dierdre's face and tried to form the words she knew she should say, feelings of betrayal and hurt swelled over her in waves.

Dierdre deserved her anger. Bradley deserved it even more, although it wasn't very productive to be angry with a man who had been dead six years. He'd never given her a chance to air her feelings as she should have when he was alive. It was righteous anger, of that she was sure. No one could possibly fault Cassie for her feelings. If only she could get Lee to understand.

"You sound so hurt and angry, Cassie. Have you taken any of this to the Lord?"

"I've tried. It almost feels like he's not listening anymore," Cassie said.

"He always listens, child," Dorothy said. "If there's a wall between you, God hasn't built it. But it is a hard thing Lee's asked of you."

"Can you talk to him? Maybe he'll understand if it comes from you." Cassie said, leaning back in her chair.

"Now, hold on, child," Miss Dorothy admonished. "I said it was a hard thing. I didn't say you shouldn't do it."

"Oh." Cassie felt her shoulders slump. "But how, Dorothy? I can't do this. There is no way on earth I could go up to Dierdre and ask her forgiveness. Right now I don't even know where she is. And even when we find her, I don't feel like I should ask. I don't have the strength."

"You don't have to have anything yourself," Dorothy said. "I don't think Lee expected you to do this alone, on your own strength. Can I tell you a story?"

"Sure," Cassie said, feeling even more puzzled than she had any time in the last two horrible days. "If you think you'll have something that will help me, I'd gladly listen."

"I know this is long distance," Dorothy said guardedly.

Cassie felt closer to laughing than she had in days. "Oh, Dorothy, this phone bill is the least of my worries right now. You just tell your story."

She could hear the answering smile in Dorothy's voice. "All right child. Settle back and listen, because here it comes. In 1937, I was seven years old, and my brother Clarence was ten, and my sister Eleanor was four. And yes, if you can do real fast addition, now you know how old I am," Dorothy said.

Cassie laughed softly and settled back to listen. The cadence of Dorothy's voice was soothing.

"We lived a pretty good life," Dorothy continued. "Granted, my folks didn't have much money. But they owned their own home, something that wasn't always the way of things for people of color in rural Missouri in those days. Daddy was a 'shade tree' mechanic. He could fix anything with an engine. I expect that had he been white, he'd have had the finest garage in town. As it was, we lived on the outskirts of a little town down in the boot heel of Southern Missouri, and he fixed cars and tractors and whatever else he could for folks outside under a big sycamore."

Dorothy painted such a vivid picture with her words that Cassie could almost see the little town and the tree Dorothy's father worked under.

"He made a good living, and Mama made sure with her vegetable garden and taking in washing and ironing if she had to that we never went without the necessities. One day during that hot summer we were going to visit Daddy's sister all the way in St. Louis. I had never been on such a grand trip before and I was very excited.

"So were Clarence and Ellie—"

"Your brother and sister?"

"Yes, dear." Dorothy chuckled. "And they were a pair. Lively. My goodness, they were lively. Anyway, as I was saying, we were good in the car. Daddy's roadster was more than ten years old, but it purred like a kitten. We got all the way to Flat River without so much as a flat tire. It was about then, though, that Mama looked back in the back seat and told Daddy he had to stop. 'Eleanor doesn't look well,' she told him."

Cassie sat forward. There was sadness now in Dorothy's tone.

"I looked at my little sister and saw that she was right. Ellie had stopped bothering me about twenty miles back, but I just figured she felt a little peaked because she got carsick on long trips. One look told me, even at seven years old, that this was something else.

"My parents stopped the car, got out, and looked at her. By then she was starting to cry and moan a little. They had a hurried conference in the front seat. Then, looking grim, my father started the car again, and we drove into the town of Flat River."

Again, Cassie noted the change in Dorothy's voice. "They stopped to find a doctor?" she asked.

"Yes, that's right. And it wasn't long before we found a sign in front of a neat brick house that proclaimed that the local doctor lived there, and even had a clinic on the premises.

"Daddy knocked at the front door. When a tall man with thinning brown hair answered, I could hear his conversation. I could also hear the man's response."

"What did he say?" Cassie asked, fearing she knew the answer.

"'I don't treat n——s,' he said. Even then that hated word made me ache."

"Oh, Dorothy," Cassie said softly.

"And we don't let your kind stay overnight around here, so don't let me hear of you hanging around, you hear?' Then he shut the door on Daddy.

"My daddy came back to the car. Clarence was mad, and I was crying. Mama looked like she wanted to cry too, but she didn't. 'You just drive on, Clifford,' she told him. 'I'll take care of Ellie the best I can.'

"Mama changed places with Clarence and me, making us sit up front with Daddy. She sat in back and crooned to Ellie, wiping her little hot face with a towel. I remember she got the water from the jug we'd brought along for our picnic lunch."

Cassie leaned forward, changing the phone to her other ear. "Did she get better?" she asked. "I mean, when you got home?"

"We didn't go home. We were closer to Daddy's sister's house in St. Louis, where there was medicine and a doctor who would help anybody. I figured the doctor would come, and look at Ellie, and then everything would be all right. That was the way it had always worked before. But it didn't work that way then."

Cassie got a sick, sinking feeling in the pit of her stomach. She almost couldn't bear for Dorothy to go on.

Dorothy cleared her throat softly. "The doctor came, all right. And suddenly Ellie was gone, taken to a hospital. Mama and Daddy were gone too, with her, and my brother and I were left behind with my aunt. She said we all needed to pray for Ellie, pray real hard.

"Mama and Daddy didn't come back until the next day, real late. Mama had been crying, and Daddy looked like someone had punched him. They said Ellie was dead, that her appendix had ruptured, and the doctors in St. Louis just couldn't do anything."

"Oh, Dorothy, I'm so sorry," Cassie said. She could hear the still-fresh pain in Dorothy's voice.

"It was a hard time, dear. I knew Ellie was with Jesus, and I was glad for her. But I missed her so, and I couldn't understand why she had to leave. I still thought about that doctor and asked Daddy a lot of questions about him. I didn't understand, in my child's mind, how anybody could turn away a sick little girl, no matter what color her skin. Especially someone trained to heal. But my daddy told me the Lord would deal with the doctor, that it wasn't our job.

"In a few weeks, it was almost time for school to start. It felt so strange to think of starting without Ellie. I still missed her so much. Most days I spent kicking my bare toes in the dirt of our yard, trying to find a substitute for all the games we'd played together. One hot day one of our neighbors' teams came down the road, a shiny Buick roadster suffering the indignity of being pulled behind the mules.

"The man who owned the car was with it. 'It just quit on me,' he said. 'Just plain old quit two miles out of town. And I have to get to Little Rock.'

"That was still a long ways away. And here he was, a white man in a nice suit, obviously with no idea of how to fix a car. But that wasn't what made me stop and stare."

"Who was it?" Cassie thought she knew.

"Daddy and the neighbor unhitched that car from behind the mules. And I stood there in open-mouthed amazement. It was the doctor from Flat River!"

"What did your father do?" Cassie said into the phone.

"My daddy proceeded to fix his car!"

"Why would he? After what happened. I can't imagine—" Cassie began, but Dorothy interrupted.

"I didn't believe it at first myself. Why wasn't Daddy hitting the man, or screaming at him? Then I thought he might do something awful to the nasty old doctor's car, something to pay him back for what he did to our sweet Ellie. But no, he just went on fixing that car the best he could.

"'What do I owe you?' the doctor asked him when he was done.

"'No charge, sir,' my Daddy said. At that I almost ran out from behind the tree where I'd been hiding. No charge! Not for the parts he'd used. Not for Daddy's hard work. No charge! My Daddy had lost his mind."

"What did the doctor say?" Cassie asked.

"'That doesn't seem right,' he said. 'And you look awfully familiar. Where do I know you from?'

"Quietly, Daddy told him. By the time he finished, the doctor looked embarrassed. 'I'm sorry,' he said. And he reached out his hand, as if to shake Daddy's hand.

"I knew what Daddy would do then. He'd call the righteous anger of the Lord down and tell the man how to repent for his terrible mistake. Daddy was a deacon in our little AME church in town, and he knew his Scripture forward and backward. I was sure he would use it now to his advantage.

"Instead, Daddy just looked at the man's hand. Then, slowly, he shook it. A short time later, the doctor got in his car and drove away. We never did see him again.

"Well, this was too much for me. I marched out from behind the tree and went straight to Daddy. 'How could you do that?' I asked him. 'How could you help that man and be nice to him after what he did to us?'

"'I didn't help him, Dot, not all by myself,' Daddy told me. 'Jesus helped that man. Jesus took my hand and reached it out to another one of his children. Because Jesus can do anything. By myself, I just wanted to spit in that man's face and let him walk back to St. Louis. But that's not what Jesus wanted him to do, I know, because my Bible tells me to love my neighbor as myself. And no matter what color his skin is, or what he's done to me, that man was my neighbor.

"'Since Jesus is the one that told me to do that,' my daddy said, 'I figured that he would help me love him.'"

Dorothy let out a deep sigh. "It was a few years more before I really understood what my Daddy was trying to teach me," she said. "He was trying to teach me about the strength that comes from our surrender to Jesus."

It wasn't until Dorothy stopped speaking that Cassie realized tears were tracing down her cheeks. In light of Dorothy's story, her own problems seemed trivial. "I understand," she said after a moment. "I think I finally understand."

"Tell me, child," Dorothy said gently, "what it is you understand."

"We need to let Jesus do those things that are too hard for us. Those things we think are impossible."

"God is so good," Dorothy said. "He led you to this place just so you would understand. So you would discover the miracle of his healing power, the miracle of his grace."

"It's the hardest place I've ever been in. The uncertainty and fear…" Her voice trailed off.

"He knows that, too. But you're not in this place alone, child. He's here with you. Holding you. Helping you."

The tears continued to flow. "Dorothy?" she said after a moment.

"Yes, dear. I'm here."

"Would you pray with me?"

"I would love to, dear. Remember, where two or three of us are gathered, he is with us, in power and might." And without another word, Dorothy began to pray as if speaking to her dearest friend. "Heavenly Father…"

Cassie took a deep breath. Bowing her head over Dierdre's table, she spoke the words that would change her life. *Heavenly Father...* she also began.

And with those words Cassie began the journey she believed, until shortly before, that she could never take.

Nineteen

Once Cassie got off the phone with Miss Dorothy, she paced and prayed some more. She drank coffee and paced a little more, until she felt she would go mad if Lee didn't show up or she didn't know soon what was happening with the children. She knew she needed to trust God in all of this, to give it to him in such a way she wouldn't be tempted to take it back. At that point she knew it was time to test this new faith.

"Lord, I've told you I will trust in you no matter what," she said out loud. "Now I'm going to go over to that nice, comfy couch over there and lie down and sleep. Dear Jesus, please let me sleep and wake refreshed and ready to look for my children."

She lay down, and when she woke, it was to a sound that first confused her, and then sent her springing from the cushions. Dierdre's garage door was going up! Cassie headed for the kitchen, still pushing her sleep-disordered hair out of her face.

She could hear the three of them in the garage, the trunk of Dierdre's car opening and closing. Then she watched the doorknob turn, and Zach burst through the door.

"I'll carry this into the den, okay, Gram?" He was carrying, not the suitcase that Cassie expected, but a box. When he saw her, he nearly dropped it. "Mom? How'd you get here? Hey, Gram, Mom's here!"

Cassie wanted to cross the few feet between them and squeeze her son until he couldn't breathe. However, that would have been out of character for the few days they'd been apart, so she held off a little. She walked the several feet and hugged him, a brief hug that filled her senses with all that she associated with Zach; curly golden hair, the sweet, pungent smell of soap and boy sweat, the softness of his hair tucked under her chin, the roughness of his jacket.

It didn't take long for Zach to squirm. "Mom? I've gotta go put down this box and get another one for Gram. We went to the Holidome on the other side of town and went swimming last night. Neat, huh? When we got up this morning we had room service breakfast, went shopping, and came home."

"That's great, Zach," she told him, trying to mean it so that he wouldn't see the panic draining from her features.

By now Sarah and Dierdre were in the doorway. Seeing her daughter, Cassie's heart leapt again. "I'll take this one in the den too, Gram. Then I'll come back and say hi, okay, Mom?"

Sarah was beautiful. There was no other word for what Cassie felt, looking at her daughter. "Okay, sweetie. See you in a minute." The children carried their boxes out, and Cassie was left alone with Dierdre. For a moment she could say nothing. Familiar anger began to well inside. She took a deep breath and offered up another silent prayer. *I will trust you in all of this, Lord.*

Dierdre stepped into her kitchen and put her black patent clutch bag on the countertop. She suddenly looked a decade older to Cassie than when she had seen her, just days before, at the mall in Columbia.

"So how did you get here?" Dierdre asked, one eyebrow

cocked. "There's no car outside."

"Lee drove me up. We came yesterday, planning to grab the children back and make a run for it. We had a bit of a disagreement last night and he went to stay at a motel. I really wish I knew where he was."

"I'm sure you do," Dierdre said.

Cassie caught her breath, awaiting the belittling words she figured would follow.

"Perhaps we could start making calls," Dierdre said, surprising her.

"Make calls? Twenty-four hours ago you were ready to seek custody of my children because of this man. Now you want to find him?" She wondered what Dierdre had up her sleeve now.

"Maybe we should sit down first." Dierdre sighed heavily as she pulled out a chair and settled into it. "There are some things I need to say to you."

Cassie sat across from her, expecting the worst. For a moment neither woman spoke. "This morning I woke up in that hotel room with the children...." Dierdre finally said. Then her voice faltered.

Cassie held her breath, bracing herself for Dierdre's usual negative, blame-twisting words.

"The woman looking back at me in the mirror was a bitter old woman," Dierdre said. "A bitter old woman bent on being vindictive and hurting you. It wasn't who I wanted to be." She sighed deeply. "It had been a long time since I'd thought about God—what he intended for me, or for these children."

"God?" Cassie managed to croak, unable to comprehend the turn this conversation was taking.

Dierdre met her gaze and nodded slowly. "Yes, God. I'm not sure I can explain it," she said, frowning. "Since the children have been with me, they've chattered about Bible stories they've heard in Sunday school and church. I only half listened, but one thing came through loud and clear. Christ has become a very important part of their lives…almost as if he is an unseen member of your household.

"Suddenly—while I was looking into the mirror—I thought about how he was once an important part of my life. A long time ago, I sought his will, but through the years, I've stubbornly gone my own way, taken matters into my own hands."

Cassie started to respond, but Dierdre held up a hand. "I did a very foolish thing, here, Cassie. More than one foolish thing. Now that I'm back home, I can't imagine what prompted me to even consider abducting my own grandchildren. And all because their mother committed the unspeakable crime of falling in love with a man who wasn't my son."

Cassie finally took a breath, aware that she'd barely dared breathe while Dierdre was speaking. This conversation she was having with Dierdre was one she would never have thought possible yesterday. "Do the children know?" she finally managed.

"No. As far as they're concerned, we went out last night to the motel for just another treat. I had planned to tell them there, but I couldn't." Dierdre's hand trembled as she reached up to touch her hair. "I'm still amazed we didn't come home to find the police ringing the house and a warrant out for my arrest. How could you be so calm?"

"Calm?" Cassie laughed. "The last thing I have been in the past forty-eight hours is calm." She hesitated, searching for the right words. "Dierdre, you're right about Christ being an unseen member of our household. I've come back to him." She sighed. "I know I don't always succeed, but I've tried to put him in charge of my life. I don't always do a good job."

"No one does, Cassie," the older woman said. "You know I haven't, either."

Here it was. The perfect opportunity for Cassie to say what

she needed to. She again prayed silently for strength. This was still too hard, too scary, for her. But not for Jesus. Opening her eyes again, she put him in charge. She pictured Miss Dorothy and heard her words again. In her mind's eye, there was that little girl being comforted by her father. And there was that earthly father who'd put his trust in a Father far greater. If they could do that, why couldn't she?

"I know," Cassie said. "And I've been so angry with you. Even before yesterday, I always felt that you hated me. That you wanted to blame me for everything that had happened to Bradley, and you were punishing me for that with all the petty little ways we agreed to disagree."

"You're probably right," Dierdre said. "It was much easier to squabble with you than it would have been to think ill of my own son. Especially when he was dead. After a while, thinking the worst of you got to be a habit, Cassie. A habit I knew was wrong in the sight of God, or even out of common decency. But it was a habit I didn't want to break."

This was running so counter to the way Cassie had played the scene over in her mind that she knew only the Lord was guiding them both. She breathed another silent prayer for guidance and went on. "It wasn't all one-sided. For so many years I've kept a mental list of all the times you've done a bad job. Every time I had to ask for money that I felt was due to the kids without asking. Every time you put down my parenting skills, or something one of them did. I carried every bit of that around like a trunk full of rocks."

Dierdre started to say something, but Cassie motioned for her not to. "That wasn't right. And I want to ask your forgiveness for not insisting we have this conversation years ago. It was easier to go on with my habit of carrying that load of anger instead of attempting to work out our differences. It was easier to blame you than to take the responsibility of reconciliation.

We could have been much better friends, and definitely allies for our children."

"It's understandable…" Dierdre began. Cassie felt an expression of pain flash across her face. Dierdre must have been able to see it too, because she stopped for a moment. "No. That's not what you need to hear, is it? This was so hard for you to do, Cassie. And you don't need to hear me tell you that I would have done the same thing."

Straightening her shoulders, Dierdre took a long, deep breath. "Of course I forgive you, Cassie. I love you, even though I have odd ways of showing it. And as long as we're getting things off our chests, I want to hear you say you forgive me as well."

"For what? Doing what you thought was right for the two most important people in the world for you?" Cassie asked. "The answer's yes, I can. I forgive you." Dierdre gave her a questioning look, and Cassie added, "With God's help, I can, Dierdre."

"Thank you." Her tense expression softened. She fell silent for a moment. "Perhaps we can start again."

"We've got a lot to work out," Cassie said.

Dierdre nodded. "I know."

"But for the children's sakes…no, make that, for our sakes…we need to try."

"I agree with you. But we've got to start sometime, someplace. Maybe today's the day."

"I'd like that, Dierdre. But how about starting again over a cup of tea? If we're going to talk this out, I could use something hot to drink."

Dierdre laughed lightly. "You have opinions after all. Let me go check on the children and see if they really know how to set up that horrid thing we bought while we were out."

"Don't tell me you got them video games," Cassie said.

"Not at all. I haven't changed that much. On Zachary's recommendation, I got something for me. A computer. Zachary assures me it will make communicating with them a snap. I'm not so sure about that. Confidentially, I'm terrified to turn the thing on. But Sarah says she'll show me how."

Cassie put the kettle on while Dierdre checked on the children. Cassie let out a shaky laugh and ran her hand through her already-disordered hair. *This isn't what I expected, Lord. Not at all. I came in here ready to do battle, to snatch up my children with nothing but the clothes on their backs and run for the border. It seems we're having tea instead.*

A few moments later Cassie and Dierdre were sitting in the kitchen drinking tea, listening to the children's voices drifting down the hall as they assembled their grandmother's new computer.

Then Cassie heard another sound above the sweet squabbling of the children. It was the slam of a car door outside. Knowing, just knowing, it was Lee, she hurried to the front door. He was halfway up the walk, and quickened his pace when she opened the door.

"Cass? I found them, at least I almost did. They spent the night at a Holidome south of town last night. So they can't have gotten far...."

"They're inside," Cassie said, walking into his embrace. "Dierdre and I are in the kitchen having a cup of tea. I would love for you to join us."

"How did you...or they...?" Still with his arms around her, Lee seemed lost for words.

"They came back on their own. With a little nudge from the Lord, perhaps. And I guess I've gotten one, too. Oh, Lee, you were so right! Forgiving Dierdre came so easily when it wasn't me doing it, when it was Jesus doing it for me and with me."

His expression was a picture, going from joy to puzzlement and back to joy again in such a brief flash. "There's a lot of story I missed out on here, I have a feeling."

Cassie reached up on tiptoe and kissed his cheek. Just feeling the roughness of the beard he hadn't scraped off this morning and the cool air on his face made her want to giggle. "There is. And I promise, I'll tell you all of it soon. But right now you'll just have to take my word for it and come in and meet Dierdre and have a cup of tea."

Still looking like he'd been hit by a Louisville slugger, Lee nodded. "Sure. Okay. Let's go." And he followed her back inside the house.

Dierdre Neel wasn't the dragon Lee expected. A little over five feet tall, she looked more like Little Red Riding Hood's grandmother than the big bad wolf. Her soft gray hair was sculpted into a short cut, and her hazel eyes were set against slightly sharp features. She wore an impeccably tailored silk shirtwaist dress in a soft green-and-blue paisley print.

The tea was Darjeeling, steeped in a pot that Lee would have guessed was Limoge, or some other extremely fine china. There was a whole tea service to match, and he felt a little rough and awkward drinking tea out of one of the thin cups. Every time he set it down in its pink-patterned saucer, he winced a little, sure it was going to shatter. He was used to hefty coffee mugs used for serving at the coffee shop halfway between Dogwood School and the police station. However, he felt he was being tested here, and it wouldn't do to be found wanting. So he continued to drink tea from a delicate cup and gently put it down each time.

"You know you scared the daylights out of Cassie," he finally said to Dierdre as she sat down with the two of them at her kitchen table. It was a far different room than Cassie's homey environment. There were lace curtains at the window, starched into knife-edged gathers. White walls, white woodwork, with a touch of blue or yellow here and there giving the only color besides shining chrome. Behind the glass fronts of the cabinets, glassware and plates were lined up with military precision. It saddened Lee somehow because he suspected little of it ever got used.

"I expect I did. That was the point," Dierdre said. "All of a sudden my grandchildren's lives seemed to be turned upside down. I wanted to do a little turning of my own."

"Well, you sure succeeded," Cassie said. "Were you serious? About keeping them here?"

"I think I was, when I talked myself into it," Dierdre said, stirring artificial sweetener into her cup. "When Zachary told me all about what had been happening at home, I was sure they were being horribly mistreated. And I was sure that no good could come out of you finding a young man."

"Especially somebody as everyday as a cop who works in a grade school," Lee put in, a little irritated by her tone.

"All right. So there was that." Dierdre looked at him, and he could see tiredness in her eyes. "It's been a long time since I lost my son. And he was all I had. I wasn't about to let go of his children. They're my only link to Bradley. I almost lost them once, and I promised myself that would never happen again."

Cassie's cup had clinked sharply into its saucer while Dierdre was speaking. "What do you mean, almost lost them once?"

"I knew what he was planning," Dierdre said, looking first down at the smooth wood grain of the table, then slowly looking up at Cassie. "He had called me and told me. How he was leaving you and the children. I think he actually thought I'd be happy. He went on and on about how this young woman he'd become…attached to…was from a wealthy family. How her background matched his more closely. How he needed to start over without the entanglements of a house in the suburbs and small children."

Her lip was curled in disdain. "My own son. I told him he was a fool, of course. Not that he listened. He hadn't listened since he was a teenager."

"Maybe if you hadn't been widowed so young," Cassie interjected. "I know what it's like now, trying to raise children alone."

"I was never widowed," Dierdre said, her chin raising as she looked straight at Cassie, daring her to react. "Bradley's father divorced me when Bradley was an infant. I was twenty years old, living with him on a military base nearly a thousand miles from home. My parents thought it would be better if I came home to Kansas City as a 'widow' instead of divorcèe in 1959. It was how things were done in those days. No one here had ever met Stephen Neel, and he made it clear he had no intention of ever contacting the two of us again. My parents had plenty of money to help support the two of us, and Stephen never failed in his responsibilities there."

Cassie looked stunned. Lee reached out and took her hand across the table. She looked at him and smiled, then looked back at Dierdre. "So Bradley was going to leave me in the same predicament your husband had left you in."

"Except you had two children and no family capable of helping. I don't mean that unkindly, but I've met your mother, Cassie. I told him I'd cut him off without a cent. He laughed again, told me that wasn't possible. That he'd researched the family trust and the way my parents had left it, and there was no way I could keep him from getting his share. Then he told me he'd made me his executor just to aggravate me if anything should happen to him. I'm ashamed to admit that at that moment I hoped terrible things would happen to him. My own son."

"Oh, Dierdre." Cassie reached out to the other woman and took her slender hands in hers. "We could have been so different all these years. I always felt that I wasn't good enough for you. And I was sure I was the only one who knew about Bradley and what he was planning."

"So he had told you. I couldn't dare say anything," Dierdre said, taking back one hand to wipe away a stray tear. "I was sure you'd keep the children from me if I told you what Bradley was planning. For a while I was able to convince myself that it had to be your fault somehow. At least it gave me an outlet for my anger."

"And that probably started all over again when you found out about me," Lee put in.

"It did," Dierdre admitted. She let go of Cassie's hands and used her crumpled tissue again then took a sip of tea. Making a face, she set down the cup. "It's cold."

"Let me boil some water and make fresh," Lee said, getting up. "I know I can boil water, and I'll admit that it's a lot easier than this conversation."

Dierdre waggled a finger at him. "Oh no you don't. You're not getting away so easily. You just sit back down here and keep talking, young man. I want to know your intentions toward my grandchildren."

"How about their mother?" Lee asked. "Wouldn't you like to know my intentions there, too?"

"I can see those already," Dierdre said, smiling for the first time since he'd met her. "And I know what the children think of you. Now I want to know what you think of them. And be careful how you answer."

What kind of miracle had God worked while Lee was gone

from this house? Here he was, at a point where he expected to be searching frantically for Cassie's kids, drinking tea and explaining his intentions to Dierdre instead. *Okay, Father. Help me out with this one.* Lee took a deep breath, waiting for the right words. A calm settled over him, and he looked at Dierdre, sitting across from him, and Cassie, sitting next to him. The answer was easy.

"There's only one way I can answer, and that's telling you the truth," Lee said, settling himself at the table again. "I love Cassie, and if it's God's will in both our lives, I'll marry her. Not tomorrow or anything, because we still have work to do. But my intentions are honorable, towards her and those kids in the other room. I won't lead any of them on with promises I can't keep."

Dierdre sat silently, regarding him with the calm of a cat. For a moment Lee could see how Cassie felt uncomfortable, being looked at the same way for years. "That's the one answer I can accept. The truth. It's something I'm not sure I got from my son for quite some time before he died." Dierdre seemed to have more to say. But whatever it was got interrupted by the children bursting into the room.

"You didn't tell us Lee was here, too," Zach said, bounding in and throwing his arms around Cassie. "Hi, Mom. Hi, Lee. Did you bring Skippy?"

Ah, the innocence of youth, Lee thought. "Not this time. He stayed home with a friend of mine."

"Is everything okay?" Sarah asked, more reserved. She stood a few feet from the table, regarding the grown-ups with some concern. She was old enough to sense the tension between them and to know, from what Cassie had told Lee earlier, that her mother setting foot in her grandmother's house was a rarity.

"It's fine now, Sarah. It's just fine," Cassie said, letting go of Zach. "How about that hug now?"

"A quick one," Sarah said. "Then I have to show Grandma how to use her new computer. We don't have to leave right away or anything, do we?" She looked between her mother and grandmother, trying to sort things out.

"No," they both answered at once, then stopped. Lee watched them watch each other.

"I think we'll take off tomorrow, if that's okay with the ladies. Can we stay here, Mrs. Neel? I can bunk with Zach."

Zach gave him a high five, and Dierdre gave him a slight but appreciative smile. "Yes, I'd love to have you stay," she said. "And your suggestion for sleeping arrangements is quite appropriate." Lee nearly choked on her words. She didn't know either of them, or their standards as an unmarried couple, very well. "And that's all I'm going to say about the matter," Dierdre added with a carefully raised brow, "because we know little pitchers have big ears."

"My ears aren't that big," Zach protested. "They just look that way because I need a haircut." The laughter in the room confused him, but it certainly made all the adults feel better. Lee felt himself relaxing for the first time since he'd scooped Cassie off her kitchen floor the night before. They might get through this yet.

Twenty

"How can I foot the bill for dinner and make you the most comfortable?" Lee asked Dierdre later that afternoon. "I know we're unexpected company, and I don't want to be a burden."

"That's thoughtful of you," Dierdre told him. Cassie was beginning to wonder if Dierdre had been abducted by aliens. This just wasn't the woman she'd done battle with for over a decade.

It was thoughtful of Lee to try to find a tactful way to ask her if she was prepared to cook for a crowd. Cassie could have told him that she probably wasn't. Dierdre was a good cook, as far as she knew. The kids never complained of starving when they came home from visiting her. But Cassie could almost bet that she hadn't been planning on supper for five tonight. "We haven't been out for ribs yet, Grandma," Zach piped up. "You told us we could go out for ribs once while we were here."

"I certainly did, because I know how you like them, and I'm not having you eat them in my kitchen, Zachary," his grandmother told him. "I've seen the way you eat ribs."

"I've never been to Kansas City before, and I have heard that it's famous for barbecue," Lee said. "Can we indulge Zach in something messy tonight, as my guests?"

"We can go have barbecue somewhere," Dierdre told him. Cassie leaned back and watched the maneuvering. This was interesting, watching the two most strong-willed people she knew try to grab a dinner check from one another. "But I can't possibly be your guest on this short notice."

"That's just the way I feel about being your guest, Mrs. Neel," Lee said smoothly. "And we are putting you out already, making up several guest rooms you hadn't counted on. Please, let me be the host tonight. You just point me towards the right place."

"I suppose," Dierdre said, with a slight sniff. "It's difficult to argue with someone who's obviously so used to getting his own way."

"That's one of the perks about carrying a nine millimeter automatic around. No one argues much," Lee said, with a wolfish grin.

"Don't ask me if he's usually like this," Cassie chimed in, before Dierdre could get out the words. "Because the answer would be yes. And often worse."

"Then why do you love me so much?" Lee asked, making her nearly spit out a mouthful of tea.

"*Moi?*" Cassie gave him a teasing smile, placing a delicate hand on her chest.

"You do, don't you, Mom?" Sarah asked. Cassie hadn't been aware that she was in the room. "Just coming back in to get another screwdriver. Not the Phillips kind," she said, rummaging through a drawer in the kitchen that Dierdre seemed to have set aside for the purpose of holding odd objects. "Grandma, we're just about ready. As soon as I get the printer cable hooked up, Zach and I can show you what this all does."

Then Sarah turned back to Cassie. "Well? You do love him, don't you?" she persisted. Why did her daughter have to pick this time, of all times, to ask such a serious question, Cassie wondered.

"Yes, I do," she told her. "Very much."

It amazed Cassie that it was Dierdre who stepped in and saved her from more of this discussion in public. "That's a private thing, Sarah. Instead of pursuing this conversation, let's go see what we can do with that computer." Cassie felt herself sagging against the chair in relief.

"Ah, alone at last," Lee said, with that wolfish grin back on his face. "Now that I have you in my clutches, you can tell me just what is going on around here." And letting her tea get cold, Cassie did just that, bursting into both laughter and tears in the process.

When she was done, Lee kissed away the tears. "That is so wonderful, Cass. Just so great."

Cassie nodded. "I think so, too. So what do we do now? It is New Year's Eve, you know."

Lee looked around the kitchen, as if running an idea through his head. "Does Dierdre ever get these kids for a holiday?"

"Not usually. It just doesn't work out," Cassie said. She'd have to admit that she'd done her best to get them back for most holidays. Sharing them with Bradley's mother for a holiday just hadn't been something she wanted to do.

"I know it's a little late, but we could still plan our own private party. While we are on our way to dinner, we could stop by a grocery store for funny hats and some ginger ale. That was always Mom's substitute for champagne for the kids. Make her part of the crew for a change."

"She's going to love you forever," Cassie said, a lump forming in her throat.

"And you? Will you love me forever?" Lee asked, tracing a finger down the side of her face, bringing a shiver up her spine.

She nodded, a flood of emotions keeping her from speaking. Just looking at him there in Dierdre's kitchen, Cassie let her love for him overwhelm her. It wasn't a new feeling, she found when she savored it. The feeling had been there awhile, hiding out in the corners of her heart.

Loving Lee was easy. He was all the things she had problems admitting she needed in her life; a strong man who admired her, who took charge when she needed support but stepped back and let her do things when she could. He didn't take any of her burdens when she needed to work through something on her own but was still there to support her. He'd never crossed her decisions regarding the children, always backing her up when there were conflicts.

Love one another as you love yourself, the words came unbidden into her mind. That was it. Lee loved her with a firm resolve that showed he loved himself and loved the Father. And as passionately as he wanted her love for himself, he wanted her to love God even more.

Loving Lee was easy. Loving God was something she was just learning to do. Oh, yes, she had come home to her heavenly Father, but like an infant, she was learning to walk with her hand in his, learning to trust him completely.

Lee knew about her struggle with trust, but he was willing to wait, his calm blue eyes promised. Cassie leaned into the kiss that he silently offered, a kiss that spoke of the same promise.

Help me love you, Lord. Help me trust you with the most precious things in my life, she offered silently, *my children…Lee…our lives together.*

And just as swiftly came the answer: *I will, beloved. All you have to do is ask.*

"I don't celebrate New Year's Eve much usually," Dierdre cocked her head, considering the issue. "But doing it on the spur of the moment? That sounds unconventional. You don't always do things conventionally though, do you, Lee? I get the feeling nonconformity is one of your strong points."

"Let's just call it flexibility, Mrs. Neel," Lee said, still working with a towelette to get barbecue sauce off himself and Zachary. "Working with kids in a drug prevention program teaches a lot of flexibility. You tend to do what works, even if it's a little off-beat."

"We couldn't possibly go home tonight. And you've never really gotten to celebrate a holiday with the kids, Dierdre," Cassie said. "Which is something I intend to change, right now."

Dierdre looked at her with surprise. "This is all right with you?"

"Oh yes," Cassie admitted. "We need to try something new once in a while. Like your computer. And having a holiday together."

"Then let's do it," Dierdre said, putting down her napkin. "I haven't planned a party on this short a notice in years, but why not?"

"Does this mean we can stay up until midnight? Two nights in a row?" Zach asked with enthusiasm.

"Sure," Cassie said. The chances that Zachary would make it up that late both nights were practically nil, so agreeing to it was a safe thing. "Are you done with your ribs?"

"I think so," Zach said. "There's nothing left to chew on."

"And no sauce left in the entire county that isn't on one of us," Lee said ruefully, still working at removing the maroon ooze. "But it was fun, wasn't it?"

"Yeah," Zach said. "Can we have ice cream for dessert?"

Lee looked at him in surprise. "Could you handle dessert right now?"

Zach's grin made Cassie laugh. "Sure. Can't you?"

"No way, pal. Maybe your grandma would agree to bringing some home for our party. Because if I have anything more now, I'm going to explode."

"I guess I can wait then," Zach said.

"Good," Sarah put in. "Because I don't want to see either of you explode at the table. Miss Manners wouldn't approve, huh, Grandma?"

"She certainly wouldn't," Dierdre said. "For that matter, neither would I."

Cassie sat back in her chair, looking at this little group in wonder. Dierdre never bantered with the children, or anyone else. Normally she wouldn't have let Zachary eat ribs, anywhere. And she certainly wouldn't have taken the one he offered halfway through dinner and tasted it herself.

But here she was, smiling indulgently and agreeing to a party on ten minute's notice. This was the same woman who had threatened, just days before, to get custody of her grandchildren. God had truly wrought a miracle in all their lives. Of course, he had a little help from Lee Winter, she thought with a smile.

Cassie was beginning to wonder if maybe she'd misjudged Dierdre all these years. That the walls of mistrust she'd built up herself, because of Bradley's betrayal, had spilled over into her relationship with his mother.

Dierdre truly cared about the children. She would have disrupted her own life on a scale Cassie could barely imagine just to make sure they were safe and well. Granted, it still rubbed Cassie the wrong way that Dierdre would consider her incapable of properly caring for her own children. But considering this well-groomed older lady across the table, she saw a different person than she'd seen before.

This person was a concerned grandmother. A lonely woman who was thrilled at the prospect of having her family together for a holiday, such a simple thing. And it had taken Lee to show this Dierdre to her.

Maybe she could start looking at things his way a little more often, Cassie thought. It certainly worked this time. She had planned on being halfway home by now, probably with upset children who'd been through the trauma of being snatched from their grandmother, but they were all planning a party instead.

"How do you feel about funny hats?" Cassie asked Dierdre.

"I still loathe them," Dierdre admitted. "I don't have a hairdresser's appointment until Tuesday, and I'm not flattening this for anybody, even Sarah and Zachary, before then."

So some things didn't change, Cassie thought. "Then we'll just have to get you an obnoxious noisemaker instead," she said, watching the surprise on Dierdre's face. Lee was right. It was fun to be unconventional. Or, how had he put it, flexible.

Flexible was good. Perhaps a little more flexibility would have prevented this situation altogether. Certainly it changed what could have been major trauma for everyone involved into just a minor blip on life's radar screen. "What about ginger ale? And ice cream and maybe even some of those awful cheese balls in a can?"

"Now those I can live with," Dierdre said, her answering grin positively wicked. "That is if you'll let me go home and put on my jogging suit. I'm so stuffed trying to keep up with Zachary that I don't think I'll wear anything with buttons for a week."

"Agreed," Cassie said. "Let me run in the grocery store on the way home to pick out ice cream. You won't believe what Zach's going to want on his."

"Try me," Dierdre said, standing up from the table. "Remember, I did raise his father. It can't be any worse than grape jelly and scrambled eggs. Have I ever told you that story?"

Dierdre as a human being, a mother having to put up with a Bradley as awful as Zach could be on his bad days. It bore thinking about. Cassie reached out to take the older woman's arm. "No, but I'd like to hear about it," she told her. "Come on, guys. Let's go party."

Flexibility. It was going to be fun. Especially when it meant leaving an amazed Lee with her two dumbfounded children at the table while she headed for the parking lot arm-in-arm with Dierdre. It was going to be plenty of fun.

Twenty-one

Cassie spent the night, what part of it she slept, on the trundle beside Sarah's frilly daybed in the guest room. It was wonderful to wake and hear her daughter's even breathing nearby. But after a few moments of listening, she knew it was time to get out of the room and let Sarah sleep.

Even though she'd stayed up past midnight with everyone else, ushering in the new year, Cassie woke up a little past seven as dawn brightened the sky. She lay in the unfamiliar bed, staring at the ceiling for a little while, but she couldn't will herself back to sleep.

"Might as well find out where Dierdre keeps the coffee," she finally said to herself, reaching for the jeans she'd taken off the night before. She hadn't packed much for this trip, not expecting it to last overnight. One clean shirt, a change of underclothes, and her toothbrush and hair supplies had been the extent of what she'd tossed into an overnight bag. And she'd already worn the shirt when they went out to dinner the night before.

She managed to make herself as presentable as possible, then went downstairs quietly in hopes everybody else would sleep in for a while.

In a moment she had a pot of coffee perking. It was nice to sit in the kitchen and watch the day start alone, yet know her family was close. The winter sunrise was pearl pink against the clouds, and Cassie wondered where she'd left her Bible after yesterday's storms. Perhaps she could pick up where she'd left off a few days earlier in Psalms. There was something about the quiet of a winter morning that made her want to start there.

Before she could get up to look for anything, Dierdre joined her in the kitchen. "I hope I didn't wake you," Cassie said. Dierdre was in a housecoat that zipped up the front, with a flannel gown peeking out from under the hem. It was the most casual attire of any kind that Cassie had ever seen her in.

"You didn't wake me. I get up this early, or earlier, every day," Dierdre said. "I see you found the coffee supplies. Are you making enough for Lee, too?"

"I am. Although I have no idea whether or not he's one of those people that has to have a cup first thing in the morning like me. The only time I've seen him this early in the morning, we had stayed up most of the night when Zach's eye got scratched, and we were both in need of serious caffeine."

Dierdre went about filling the tea kettle and putting it on the stove. "He seems like a good man."

"I'm glad you think so," Cassie said, really meaning it. There was such a difference in her feelings toward the older woman since she'd asked God to take them over. Still, there was one thing she wanted to know. "Dierdre, I have to ask. What changed your mind about keeping the kids?" she finally blurted out, asking the question that had been on her mind since the previous day.

"Zachary," Dierdre said, sitting down with her tea cup to wait for her water to boil. "He's a wonderful child, Cassie. Not that Sarah isn't. But sometimes I think I favor her because I never had a little girl. Zachary is so much his father all over

210

again, in the wonderful ways…" she smiled, remembering, "…all the ways that drove me insane when I was raising Bradley." She looked down at her cup for a moment, then again met Cassie's gaze. "Yesterday morning I planned to tell them what I was going to do. I had all my arguments lined up and everything."

Cassie felt confused. "And Zach changed your mind? He didn't even seem aware of any of this when we came yesterday."

"I don't think he was," Dierdre said. "When I woke up in the motel room, he was already awake. When he saw that I was too, he bounded over to my bed from the desk where he'd been sitting, with a sketch in his hand. He'd woken up hours before the rest of us, apparently, and spent his time drawing. I've encouraged that, I suppose."

"Good," Cassie said. "I try to keep him quiet for a while in the morning so that Sarah and I don't have to get up before dawn. What had he drawn for you?"

"A shirt," Dierdre said, looking bemused. "He told me it was the design his class had chosen for their DARE shirts. Then he explained what DARE was, and how each class got to pick out their own logo for a shirt for their 'graduation' and such. And every third sentence was 'Lee says' this and 'Lee thinks' that. And as I listened to him, I realized how important Lee was to his life. And here I was about to pull him away from the one male support he had. He's just at the age where I found it nearly impossible to raise his father alone. It made my worries about his staying with you look very, very foolish."

"So you didn't tell them?" Cassie felt her eyes filling up with grateful tears.

"Neither of them. And I hope you won't either. We all make mistakes, and I almost made the same big one twice." Then she laughed softly. "Of course I may have made one every bit as big getting this computer and promising to get them one as well."

211

"I wondered about that part," Cassie admitted. "They could always use the lab at school for now to send you e-mail, but I didn't think their limited time in there for such things would suffice."

"It won't. And I hope you won't hesitate to go shopping for the right machine and tell me what it's going to cost. Sarah assures me that right after Christmas is a great time to buy."

"She's right," Cassie said, holding back the arguments she could have made about things the children needed much more than a computer. "If you really want me to, we'll start looking when we get home."

"I really do," Dierdre said. "And I expect a note from you once in a while too, not just from the children."

"Consider it done," Cassie said, sipping her coffee and marveling again at the strange ways her life had turned around lately. She was cheerfully taking money from Dierdre and promising to write. There was more that was new to today than the pale pink clouds that were shining outside the kitchen window.

When it was time to leave Dierdre's, Cassie found herself wishing she could stay longer for the first time in her life. Once more she offered up a silent prayer of thanks for this change in feelings only God could have brought about.

"We'll get our computer tomorrow after school, Gram," Zach promised. "You'll take us, won't you, Mom?"

"Sure. Otherwise how could Gram write you? And you write back?" she asked, ruffling his hair.

"And remember, Cassie, you're to write, too. Not just the children," Dierdre said. "I expect you'll have some news for me soon."

Smiling, Cassie didn't know quite how to answer her. "That depends on things that aren't in my control, Dierdre," she said softly as she hugged the older woman good-bye. "But I hope so. I truly hope so."

"Well, keep me posted," Dierdre said. "I want to plan my trip."

"You should plan a trip no matter what. We'd love to have you," Cassie said. And meant every word of it.

"I will," Dierdre said, seeming to surprise herself as much as anybody else. "And you drive safely, Lee. Take care of my family."

"I will, Mrs. Neel," he said, giving her a quick hug as well. To Cassie it seemed there was a promise that passed between the two of them that was much more involved than just a highway trip.

"This was a good idea," Cassie told Lee about halfway home. "Did you figure they'd sleep most of the trip if they stayed up until midnight last night?"

"Let's just call it a wonderful side benefit," Lee said. "Should I stop to switch drivers here?"

Cassie looked back into the back seat, where both kids were using backpacks or stuffed animals as pillows and sleeping so soundly that Zach had his mouth wide open and Sarah had slumped over in the seat.

"If you don't mind driving, keep going," she told Lee. "If we stop, they'll wake up. And it's so peaceful right now. This is the first trip back from Kansas City that I've ever listened to music instead of 'she did it first.'"

"And we're already to Columbia," Lee said, sounding cheerful. "Sure you don't want to stop for a while?"

"I'd just as soon keep going," Cassie said truthfully. "The sooner we get home, the sooner I can start in on the four thousand things I have to do before school tomorrow. There's probably five loads of laundry, and my class plans, and I know we're out of bread and milk.... Lee, why are we stopping?"

Cassie had been so involved in her plans for the day ahead

that she hadn't noticed Lee turning off at a highway rest stop and pulling into a space until they were parked. "Because I can't drive and talk at the same time. Not like this, Cass." He turned in his seat to face her.

Time took on a different quality as Lee looked into her eyes. Even though Cassie knew they were surrounded by families piling in and out of the rest stop, and big tractor trailer trucks with their whoosh of air brakes, for a moment there was just Lee. His dark hair was rumpled, and his face wore a hopeful expression.

"I didn't sleep much last night, Cass. Instead, I spent most of the time talking to God. And listening, more than I talked."

A shiver went up Cassie's spine. "And what did you hear?"

"That I had to say something to you. Something about this love in my heart. I know I haven't taken you home to meet the family yet. And we haven't gone to meet your mother...."

She touched his lips to quiet him. "But you introduced me to Someone even more important, Lee. I've gotten to know my heavenly Father again. And that's so important that everything else pales in comparison. Lee Winter, I can't thank you enough for what you've done in my life," Cassie said, as Lee reached for her hands. His hands were warm and strong. A good place to entrust her heart, her life.

"So will you marry me, Cass?" he asked. His voice was soft and husky.

"Oh yes," she breathed. "Oh yes!" She lifted his hands and kissed his tapered fingertips. When she met his eyes again, they seemed almost to shimmer through her tears. "I love you," she whispered.

"I love you, Cassie," he whispered. "And I can't imagine any more wonderful life than having you, and your kids, be a part of it every day." He grew serious for a moment. "You know I'm a police officer. There are so many dangers...." His voice faltered.

Cassie sat silently for a moment, still holding Lee's hands. She knew he referred to the moment all law enforcement officer's wives feared. That knock on the door, the devastating news that might follow. "You walked into my life so long ago and gave me news I wasn't ready for. I don't believe God would do that to me again." She drew in a deep breath. "But if that's his plan for us someday, we'll just have to leave it in his hands with everything else."

Lee's voice was soft with awe. "Do you mean that, Cassie? Can you do that?"

"He can do that. I can only ask him to help me. Look at what he's done in my life already. How could I possibly not want to marry you and share your life, it that's his will for us?"

Behind them in the back seat, Cassie could hear the children, awake now, whispering to each other. "Do you think he's going to kiss her?" Zach whispered.

Lee turned around and winked at him. "Yeah, he is," he whispered back, making both children laugh. And then he turned again to Cassie, and her heart leapt as he gathered her into his arms. This was where she belonged, and she savored the feeling of happiness that sang through her entire being. Then Lee's lips found hers. It was a kiss that kept so many promises.

Twenty-two

Six months later

I'm scared again, Lord, Cassie prayed silently. The music was playing in the church, and the center aisle looked a thousand miles long. There were so many faces thronged in the pews, and they all turned to watch her as she stepped into place.

Her pale pink dress was modest, street length. Sarah insisted that she wear rosebuds in her hair on a clip, if she wouldn't agree to a veil. Sarah's own dress matched her mother's in style and was a paler pink, with matching rosebuds at the wrist.

Zach wore his rose on the lapel of the tux that he said itched and poked horribly. "How can Lee stand this thing?" he whispered. "He's got to be going nuts up there."

His aggravated whisper snapped Cassie out of her little panic. "He's just fine," she whispered back. "Just look at him."

It was true. Lee was fine, standing in front of the church in his tuxedo, dark hair gleaming and eyes shining, focused only on her.

Gazing at Lee, she wasn't nervous anymore. She wasn't scared. There was only Lee and his love, warm and welcoming, waiting for her at the end of the aisle. "Let's go," she told the kids. They each took a hand, Sarah on her right, Zach on her left.

Friends and family had crowded into the sanctuary, and now they stood as Cassie began to move slowly down the aisle. Lee's family took up three pews in the front, his father standing beside him as his best man, looking almost as proud and happy as his son.

On Cassie's side, there were three women smiling and sharing linen hankies for the inevitable tears she knew they'd all shed before the ceremony was over. Her own mother didn't argue a bit with sharing the space with Dierdre, who looked elegant in her tailored lavender suit, and Dorothy, who looked positively regal as usual in her maroon dress. As she passed them, they all gave her little nods or winks of encouragement. Her mothers, spiritual and natural, were all there to wish her well.

Lee stood in front of the pastor, watching her with a boyish look that said he could hardly wait for her to join him. Cassie stopped where they'd agreed to at the rehearsal, and the pastor began to speak. "We are gathered here today to join this couple, Lee Winter and Cassie Neel, in holy matrimony. Who gives this woman to be wed?"

In the moment before he spoke, Cassie was filled with the feeling that Zach was going to be incredibly Zachlike again. For a moment she worried, but she let the feeling pass quickly. Nothing could mar this moment, nothing was supposed to. She could feel the Spirit of love so strongly in this place that whatever happened was right.

"Who gives this woman?" the pastor asked again gently, sure that Zach had forgotten his line.

Zach squirmed a little, then piped up at last. "Well, Pastor, I really think God does, but you told me to say 'my sister and I,' so that's what I'll say."

The church erupted in laughter, which Lee and Cassie joined. Cassie leaned down quickly and brushed a kiss on Zach's uncomfortable, grimacing face. "You did fine. Now you can sit down," she whispered to both children.

"Zach, my friend, you're absolutely right," the pastor told him, motioning Cassie forward. "God does. And I guess we better get on with what he had in mind."

Cassie stepped forward to join Lee and to make her promises to him before the Father who had so miraculously brought them together. Lee took her hand, and in his touch she was welcomed home to the place where the rest of their lives would begin.

Dear Readers,

With this book I feel like someone has thrown me a giant "welcome home" party. While I've been writing, and selling, romances for the better part of a decade, this is my first book for a Christian publishing house, and I love it! My only hope is that you have half as much fun reading it as I did writing it.

If asked what gifts God has given me, "writing" and "story-telling" would come off my tongue first. Through all the crazy jobs I strung together while trying to find out just what God intended me to do with my life, writing in some form or another has always been my joy. It was only fourteen years ago, while holding my first son during one of those nights rocking a baby that seem to go on forever at the time, that God planted the seed that maybe, just maybe, I ought to try to make a living at writing.

To say that I've never doubted the wisdom of that idea would be an outright lie. But few things beat having a kinder-gartner take "Mom's first book" for show and tell. Or having a teenager who will break his normal code of silence toward parents at the mall to admit that that's his mom signing books over there.

Lee and Cassie's story is one I've wanted to tell for a long time. While all my "time" at our local grade school has been strictly volunteer, there are many programs there dear to my heart, the DARE program among them. To be able to write about it while having such a good time was a pleasure.

Yours in Christ,

Lynn Bulock

PALISADES...PURE ROMANCE

Glory, Marilyn Kok
Sierra, Shari MacDonald
Forget-Me-Not, Shari MacDonald
Diamonds, Shari MacDonald
Stardust, Shari MacDonald
Westward, Amanda MacLean
Stonehaven, Amanda MacLean
Everlasting, Amanda MacLean
Promise Me the Dawn, Amanda MacLean
Kingdom Come, Amanda MacLean
Betrayed, Lorena McCourtney
Escape, Lorena McCourtney
Dear Silver, Lorena McCourtney
Enough! Gayle Roper
Voyage, Elaine Schulte

✦ ANTHOLOGIES ✦

A Christmas Joy, Darty, Gillenwater, MacLean
Mistletoe, Ball, Hicks, McCourtney
A Mother's Love, Bergren, Colson, MacLean
Silver Bells, Bergren, Krause, MacDonald (October, 1997)